"Nathan, is there some woman I should be concerned about?"

He didn't pull away, though he knew he should. Somehow his fingers had twined with hers and were holding on. "What do you mean?"

"I mean, you said you weren't *involved*, but I wondered if...if there was someone. I don't mind competing; I'd just like to know."

There was no one. Even if there had been, her memory would have vanished like a puff of smoke. That's what worried him. "Jack, you're taking two steps to my one."

"Am I?" She shifted. It took only a small movement to have her lips whisper against his. She didn't press, content for now with simply a taste. "How long do you think it'll take you to catch up?"

Dear Reader,

Among the stellar authors in our January lineup is Lynda Trent, well-known for her weighty historical novels. What keeps her coming back to Silhouette **Special Edition**? Here's how she explains it:

"I write for Silhouette Special Edition to share a romantic fantasy with my readers, an emotional adventure in which a woman might be an heiress, a commoner or a Mata Hari . . . and still be loved by the perfect man. Within the broad scope of a Special Edition, she might dare to love a dangerous man; she might chance everything for a noble cause. I want to weave a tapestry of romance blossoming, of dreams fulfilled, and I want to share it with other dreamers."

Like the piratical hero of Lynda Trent's *Like Strangers*, the authors and editors of Silhouette **Special Edition** want to knock on the door to your heart . . . and open it to all the possibilities life and love have to offer.

Share your tastes and preferences with us. Each and every month we strive to offer you something new, something *special*. Let us know how we're doing!

Happy new year,

Leslie Kazanjian, Senior Editor
Silhouette Books
300 East 42nd Street
New York, N.Y. 10017

NORA ROBERTS
Loving Jack

Silhouette Special Edition

Published by Silhouette Books New York

America's Publisher of Contemporary Romance

To Kasey Michaels,
because Jack is a heroine she'll understand.

SILHOUETTE BOOKS
300 East 42nd St., New York, N.Y. 10017

ISBN: 0-373-09499-X

First Silhouette Books printing January 1989

Printed in the U.S.A.

Books by Nora Roberts

Silhouette Special Edition

The Heart's Victory #59
Reflections #100
Dance of Dreams #116
First Impressions #162
The Law Is a Lady #175
Opposites Attract #199
*Playing the Odds #225
*Tempting Fate #235
*All the Possibilities #247
*One Man's Art #259
Summer Desserts #271
Second Nature #288
One Summer #306
Lessons Learned #318
A Will and a Way #345
*For Now, Forever #361
Local Hero #427
°The Last Honest Woman #451
°Dance to the Piper #463
°Skin Deep #475
Loving Jack #499

*MacGregor Series

°The O'Hurleys!

Silhouette Intimate Moments

Once More with Feeling #2
Tonight and Always #12
This Magic Moment #25
Endings and Beginnings #33
A Matter of Choice #49
Rules of the Game #70
The Right Path #85
Partners #94
Boundary Lines #114
Dual Image #123
The Art of Deception #131
†Affaire Royale #142
Treasures Lost, Treasures Found #150
Risky Business #160
Mind Over Matter #185
†Command Performance #198
†The Playboy Prince #212
Irish Rose #232
The Name of the Game #264

†Cordina's Royal Family

Silhouette Christmas Stories 1986

"Home for Christmas"

NORA ROBERTS

"Those of you who have read my books in the past know that I often find it hard to resist certain characters and end up giving them a story of their own. Cody Johnson, though he only appears briefly in this story, was irresistible. I hope you'll look for him in *Best Laid Plans* in March."

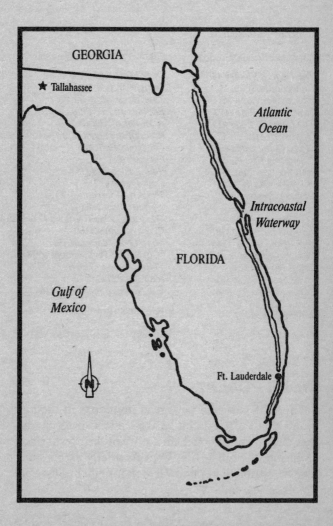

Chapter One

The minute Jackie saw the house, she was in love. Of course, she acknowledged, she did fall in love easily. It wasn't that she was easily impressed, she was just open, wide-open, to emotions—her own and everyone else's.

The house had a lot of emotion in it, she felt, and not all of it serene. That was good. Total serenity would have been all right for a day or two, but boredom would have closed in. She preferred the contrasts here, the strong angles and arrogant juts of the corners, softened occasionally by curving windows and unexpectedly charming archways.

The white-painted walls glittered in the sunlight, set off by stark ebony trim. Though she didn't believe the world was black-and-white, the house made the statement that the two opposing forces could live together in harmony.

The windows were wide, welcoming the view from both east and west, while skylights let in generous slices of sun. Flowers grew in profusion in the side garden and in terra-cotta pots along the terraces. She enjoyed the bold color they added, the touch of the exotic and lush. They'd have to be tended, of course— and religiously, if the heat continued and the rain didn't come. She didn't mind getting dirty, though, especially if there was a reward at the end.

Through wide glass doors she looked out at the crystalline waters of a kidney-shaped tiled pool. That, too, would require tending, but that, too, offered rewards. She could already picture herself sitting beside it, watching the sun set with the scent of flowers everywhere. Alone. That was a small hitch, but one she was willing to accept.

Beyond the pool and the sloping slice of lawn was the Intracoastal Waterway. Its waters were dark, mysterious, but even as she watched a motorboat putted by. She discovered she liked the sound of it. It meant there were people close enough to make contact but not so close as to interfere.

The water roads reminded her of Venice and a particularly pleasant month she had spent there during her teens. She'd ridden in gondolas and flirted with dark-eyed men. Florida in the spring wasn't as romantic as Italy, but it suited her just fine.

"I love it." She turned back to the wide, sun-washed room. There were twin sofas the color of oatmeal on a steel-blue carpet. The rest of the furniture was an elegant ebony and leaned toward the masculine. Jackie approved of its strength and style. She rarely wasted her time looking for flaws and was willing to accept them when they jumped out at her. But in this house and everything about it she saw perfection.

She beamed at the man standing casually in front of the white marble fireplace. The hearth had been cleaned and swept and was a home for a potted fern. The man's tropical-looking white pants and shirt might have been chosen for precisely that pose. Knowing Frederick Q. MacNamara as she did, Jackie was sure it had been.

"When can I move in?"

Fred's smile lit up his round, boyish face. No one looking at it would have been reminded of a shark. "That's our Jack, always going on impulse." His body was rounded, too—not quite fat, but not really firm, either. Fred's favorite exercise was hailing—cabs or waiters. He moved toward her with a languid grace that had once been feigned but was now second nature. "You haven't even seen the second floor."

"I'll see it when I unpack."

"Jack, I want you to be sure." He patted her cheek—older, more experienced cousin to young scatterbrain. She didn't take offense. "I'd hate for you to regret this in a day or two. After all, you're proposing to live in this house by yourself for three months."

"I've got to live somewhere." She gestured, palm out, with a hand as slim and delicate as the rest of her. Gold and colored stones glittered on four fingers, a sign of her love of the pretty. "If I'm going to be serious about writing, I should be alone. Since I don't think I'd care for a garret, why shouldn't it be here?"

She paused a moment. It never paid to be too casual with Fred, cousin or not. Not that she didn't like him. Jackie had always had a soft spot for Fred, though she knew he had a habit of skimming off the top and dealing from the bottom.

"You're sure it's all right for you to sublet it to me?"

"Perfectly." His voice was as smooth as his face. Whatever wrinkles Fred had were carefully camouflaged. "The owner only uses it as a winter home, and then only sporadically. He prefers having someone in residence rather than leaving it empty. I told Nathan I'd take care of things until November, but then this business in San Diego came up, and it can't be put off. You know how it is, darling."

Jackie knew exactly how it was. With Fred, "sudden business" usually meant he was avoiding either a jealous husband or the law. Despite his unprepossessing looks, he had constant problems with the former, and not even a prepossessing family name could always protect him from the latter.

She should have been warier, but Jackie wasn't always wise, and the house—the look, the feel, of it— had already blinded her.

"If the owner wants it occupied, I'm happy to accommodate him. Let me sign on the dotted line, Fred. I want to unpack and spend a couple of hours in the pool."

"If you're sure." He was already drawing a paper from his pocket. "I don't want a scene later—like the time you bought my Porsche."

"You failed to tell me the transmission was held together with Krazy Glue."

"Let the buyer beware," Fred said mildly, and handed her a monogrammed silver pen.

She had a quick flash of trepidation. This was cousin Fred, after all. Fred of the easy deal and the can't-miss investment. Then a bird flew into the garden and begin to sing cheerily, and Jackie took it as an omen. She signed the lease in a bold, flowing hand before drawing out her checkbook.

"A thousand a month for three months?"

"Plus five hundred damage deposit," Fred added.

"Right." She supposed she was lucky dear cousin Fred wasn't charging her a commission. "Are you leaving me a number, an address or something so I can get in touch with the owner if necessary?"

Fred looked blank for a moment, then beamed at her. It was that MacNamara smile, charming and guileless. "I've already told him about the turnover. Don't worry about a thing, sweetie. He'll be in touch with you."

"Fine." She wasn't going to worry about details. It was spring, and she had a new house, a new project. New beginnings were the best thing in the world. "I'll take care of everything." She touched a large Chinese urn. She'd begin by putting fresh flowers in it. "Will you be staying tonight, Fred?"

The check was already stashed in the inside pocket of his jacket. He resisted the urge to add a loving pat. "I'd love to hang around, indulge in some family gossip, but since we've got everything squared away, I should catch a flight to the Coast. You'll need to get to the market pretty soon, Jack. There're some essentials in the kitchen, but not much else." As he spoke, he started across the room toward a pile of baggage.

It never occurred to him to offer to take his cousin's bags upstairs for her, or for her to ask him to. "Keys are there on the table. Enjoy yourself."

"I will." When he hefted his cases, she walked over to open the door for him. She'd meant her invitation to spend the night sincerely, and she was just as sincerely glad he'd refused. "Thanks, Fred. I really appreciate this."

"My pleasure, darling." He leaned down to exchange a kiss with her. Jackie got a whiff of his expensive cologne. "Give my love to the family when you talk to them."

"I will. Safe trip, Fred." She watched him walk out to a long, lean convertible. It was white, like his suit. After stowing his cases, Fred scooted behind the wheel and sent her a lazy salute. Then she was alone.

Jackie turned back to the room and hugged herself. She was alone, and on her own. She'd been there before, of course. She was twenty-five, after all, and had taken solo trips and vacations, had her own apartment and her own life. But each time she started out with something new it was a fresh adventure.

As of this day...was it March 25, 26? She shook her head. It didn't matter. As of this day, she was beginning a new career. Jacqueline R. MacNamara, novelist.

It had a nice ring, she thought. The first thing she was going to do was unpack her new typewriter and begin Chapter One. With a laugh, she grabbed the typewriter case and her heaviest suitcase and started upstairs.

* * *

It didn't take long to acclimate herself, to the South, to the house, to her new routine. She rose early, enjoying the morning quiet with juice and a piece of toast—or flat cola and cold pizza, if that was handier. Her typing improved with practice, and by the end of the third day her machine was humming nicely. She would break in the afternoon to have a dip in the pool, lie in the sun and think about the next scene, or plot twist.

She tanned easily and quickly. It was a gift Jackie attributed to the Italian great-grandmother who had breached the MacNamara's obsessively Irish ranks. The color pleased her, and most of the time she remembered the face creams and moisturizers that her mother had always touted. "Good skin and bone structure make a beauty, Jacqueline. Not style or fashion or clever makeup," she'd often declared.

Well, Jackie had the skin and bone structure, though even her mother had to admit she would never be a true beauty. She was pretty enough, in a piquant, healthy sort of way. But her face was triangular rather than oval, her mouth wide rather than bowed. Her eyes were just a shade too big, and they were brown. The Italian again. She hadn't inherited the sea green or sky blue that dominated the rest of her family. Her hair was brown, as well. During her teens she'd experimented with rinses and streaks, often to her mother's embarrassment, but had finally settled for what God had given her. She'd even come to like it, and the fact that it curled on its own meant she didn't have to spend precious time in salons. She kept it short, and its natural fullness and curl made a halo around her face.

She was glad of its length now, because of her afternoon dips. It only took a few shakes and a little finger-combing to make it spring back to its casual style.

She took each morning as it came, diving headfirst into writing after she woke, then into the pool each afternoon. After a quick forage for lunch, she went back to her machine and worked until evening. She might play in the garden then, or sit and watch the boats or read on the terrace. If the day had been particularly productive, she would treat herself to the whirlpool, letting the bubbling water and the sultry heat of the glass enclosure make her pleasantly tired.

She locked the house for the owner's benefit rather than for her own safety. Each night Jackie slipped into bed in the room she'd chosen with perfect peace of mind and the tingling excitement of what the next morning would bring.

Whenever her thoughts turned to Fred, she smiled. Maybe the family was wrong about Fred after all. It was true that more than once he'd taken some gullible relative for a ride down a one-way street and left him—or her—at a dead end. But he'd certainly done her a good turn when he'd suggested the house in Florida. On the evening of the third day, Jackie lowered herself into the churning waters of the spa and thought about sending cousin Fred some flowers.

She owed him one.

He was dead tired, and happy as hell to be home at last. The final leg of the journey had seemed interminable. Being on American soil again after six months hadn't been enough. When Nathan had landed in New York, the first real flood of impatience had struck. He was home, yet not home. For the first time in months he had allowed himself to think of his own house, his own bed. His own private sacrosanct space.

Then there had been an hour's delay that had left him roaming the airport and almost grinding his teeth. Even once he'd been airborne he hadn't been able to stop checking and rechecking his watch to see how much longer he had to hang in the sky.

The airport in Fort Lauderdale still wasn't home. He'd spent a cold, hard winter in Germany and had had enough of the charm of snow and icicles. The warm, moist air and the sight of palms only served to annoy him, because he wasn't quite there yet.

He'd arranged to have his car delivered to the airport, and when he'd finally eased himself into the familiar interior he'd felt like himself again. The hours of flying from Frankfurt to New York no longer mattered. The delays and impatience were forgotten. He was behind the wheel, and twenty minutes from pulling into his own driveway. When he went to bed that night it would be between his own sheets. Freshly laundered and turned back by Mrs. Grange, who Fred MacNamara had assured him would have the house ready for his arrival.

Nathan felt a little twist of guilt about Fred. He knew he'd hustled the man along to get him up and out of the house before his arrival, but after six months of intense work in Germany he wasn't in the mood for a houseguest. He'd have to be sure to get in touch with Fred and thank him for keeping an eye on things. It was an arrangement that had solved a multitude of problems with little fuss. As far as Nathan was concerned, the less fuss the better. He definitely owed Frank MacNamara a very large thank-you.

In a few days, Nathan thought as he slipped his key into the lock. After he'd slept for twenty hours and indulged in some good, old-fashioned sloth.

Nathan pushed open the door, hit the lights and just looked. Home. It was so incredibly good to be home, in the house he'd designed and built, among things chosen for his own taste and comfort.

Home. It was exactly as he—no, it wasn't exactly as he'd left it, he realized quickly. Because his eyes were gritty with fatigue, he rubbed them as he studied the room. His room.

Who had moved the Ming over to the window and stuck irises in it? And why was the Meissen bowl on the table instead of the shelf? He frowned. He was a meticulous man, and he could see a dozen small things out of place.

He'd have to speak to Mrs. Grange about it, but he wasn't going to let a few annoyances spoil his pleasure at being home.

It was tempting to go straight to the kitchen and pour himself something long and cold, but he believed in doing first things first. Hefting his cases, he walked upstairs, relishing each moment of quiet and solitude.

He flipped on the lights in his bedroom and stopped short. Very slowly, he lowered the suitcases and walked to the bed. It wasn't turned down, but made up haphazardly. His dresser, the Chippendale he'd picked up at Sotheby's five years before, was crowded with pots and bottles. There was a definite scent here, not only from the baby roses that had been stuck in the Waterford—which belonged in the dining room cabinet—but a scent of woman. Powder, lotion and oil. Neither strong nor rich, but light and intrusive. His eyes narrowed when he saw the swatch of color on the spread. Nathan picked up the thin, almost microscopic bikini panties.

Mrs. Grange? The very idea was laughable. The sturdy Mrs. Grange wouldn't be able to fit one leg inside that little number. If Fred had had a guest... Nathan turned the panties over under the light. He supposed he could tolerate Fred having had a companion, but not in his room. And why in hell weren't her things packed and gone?

He got an image. It might have been the architect in him that enabled him to take a blank page or an empty lot and fill it completely in his mind. He saw a tall, slim woman, sexy, a little loud and bold. Ready to party. A redhead, probably, with lots of teeth and a rowdy turn of mind. That was fine for Fred, but the agreement had been that the house was to be empty and back in order on Nathan's return.

He gave the bottles on his dresser one last glance. He'd have Mrs. Grange dispose of them. Without thinking, he stuffed the thin piece of nylon in his pocket and strode out to see what else wasn't as it should be.

Jackie, her eyes shut and her head resting on the crimson edge of the spa, sang to herself. It had been a particularly good day. The tale was spinning out of her head and onto the page so quickly it was almost scary.

She was glad she'd picked the West for her setting, old Arizona, desolate, tough, dusty and full of grit. That was just the right backdrop for her hard-bitten hero and her primly naive heroine.

They were already bumping along the rocky road to romance, though she didn't think even they knew it yet. She loved being able to put herself back in the 1800s, feeling the heat, smelling the sweat. And of course there was danger and adventure at every step. Her convent-raised heroine was having a devil of a time, but she was coping. Strong. Jackie couldn't have written about a weak-minded woman if she'd had to.

And her hero. Just thinking about him made her smile. She could see him perfectly, just as if he'd popped out of her imagination into the tub with her. That dark black hair, thick, glinting red in the sun when he removed his hat. Long enough that a woman could get a handful of it. The body lean and hard from riding, brown from the sun, scarred from the trouble he never walked away from.

You could see that in his face, a lean, bony face that was often shadowed by the beard he didn't bother to shave. He had a mouth that could smile and make a woman's heart pump fast. Or it could tighten and send shivers of fear up a man's spine. And his eyes. Oh, his eyes were a wonder. Slate gray and fringed by long, dark lashes, crinkled at the corners from squinting into the Arizona sun. Flat and hard when he pulled the trigger, hot and passionate when he took a woman.

Every woman in Arizona was in love with Jake Redman. And Jackie was pleased to be a little in love with him herself. Didn't that make him real? she thought as the bubbles swirled around her. If she could see him so clearly, and feel for him this intensely, didn't it mean she was doing the job right? He wasn't a good man, not through and through. It would be up to the heroine to mine the gold from him, and accept the rough stones along with it. And boy, was he going to give Miss Sarah Conway a run for her money. Jackie could hardly wait to sit down with them so that they could show her what happened next. If she concentrated hard enough, she could almost hear him speak to her.

"What in the hell are you doing?"

Still dreaming, Jackie opened her eyes and looked into the face of her imagination. Jake? she thought, wondering if the hot water had soaked into her brain. Jake didn't wear suits and ties, but she recognized the look that meant he was about to draw and fire. Her mouth fell open and she stared.

His hair was shorter, but not by much, and the shadow of beard was there. She pressed her fingers to her eyes and got chlorine in them, then blinked them open. He was still there, a little closer now. The sound of the spa's motor seemed louder as it filled her head.

"Am I dreaming?"

Nathan's eyes narrowed. She wasn't the rowdy redhead he'd pictured, but a cute, doe-eyed brunette. Either way, she didn't belong in his house. "What you're doing is trespassing. Now who the hell are you?"

The voice. Good grief, even the voice was right. Jackie shook her head and struggled to get a grip on herself. This was the twentieth century, and no matter how real her characters seemed on paper, they didn't come to life in five-hundred-dollar suits. The simple fact was that she was alone with a stranger and in a very vulnerable position.

She wondered how much she remembered from her karate course, then took another look at the man's broad shoulders and decided it just wasn't going to be enough.

"Who are you?" The edge of fear gave her voice haughty, rounded tones her mother would have been proud of.

"You're the one who has questions to answer," he countered. "But I'm Nathan Powell."

"The architect? Oh, I've admired your work. I saw the Ridgeway Center in Chicago, and . . ." She started to scoot up, no longer afraid, but then she remembered she hadn't bothered to put on a suit and slumped back again. "You have a marvelous flair for combining aesthetics with practicality."

"Thanks. Now—"

"But what are you doing here?"

His eyes narrowed again, and for the second time Jackie saw something of her gunslinger in them. "That's my question. This is my house."

"Yours?" She rubbed the back of her wrist over her eyes as she tried to think. "You're Nathan? Fred's Nathan?" Relieved, she smiled again. "Well, that explains things."

A dimple appeared at the corner of her mouth when she smiled. Nathan noticed it, then ignored it. He was a fastidious man, and fastidious men didn't come home to find strange women in their tubs. "Not to me. I'm going to repeat myself. Who the hell are you?"

"Oh. Sorry. I'm Jack." When his brow rose, she smiled again and extended a wet hand. "Jackie—Jacqueline MacNamara. Fred's cousin."

He glanced at her hand, and at the glitter of jewels on it, but didn't take it in his. He was afraid that if he did he might just haul her out onto the tiled floor. "And why, Miss MacNamara, are you sitting in my spa, and sleeping in my bed?"

"Is that your room? Sorry, Fred didn't say which I was to take, so I took the one I liked best. He's in San Diego, you know."

"I don't give a damn where he is." He'd always been a patient man. At least that was what he'd always believed. Right now, though, he was finding he had no patience at all. "What I want to know is why you're in my house."

"Oh, I sublet it from Fred. Didn't he get ahold of you?"

"You what?"

"You know, it's hard to talk with this motor running. Wait." She held up a hand before he could hit the Off button. "I'm, ah . . . well, I wasn't expecting anyone, so I'm not exactly dressed for company. Would you mind?"

He glanced down automatically to where the water churned hot and fast at the subtle curve of her breast. Nathan set his teeth. "I'll be in the kitchen. Make it fast."

Jackie let out a long breath when she was alone. "I think Fred did it again," she muttered as she hauled herself out of the tub and dried off.

Nathan made himself a long gin and tonic, using a liberal hand with the gin. As far as homecomings

went, this one left a lot to be desired. There might have
been men who'd be pleasantly surprised to come home
after an exhausting project and find naked women
waiting in their sun rooms. Unfortunately, he just
wasn't one of them. He took a deep drink as he leaned
back against the counter. It was, he supposed, just a
question of taking one step at a time—and the first
would be disposing of Jacqueline MacNamara.

"Mr. Powell?"

He glanced over to see her step into the kitchen. She
was still dripping a bit. Her legs were lightly tanned
and long—very long, he noticed—skimmed at the
thighs by a terry-cloth robe that was as boldly striped
as Joseph's coat of many colors. Her hair curled
damply around her face in a soggy halo, with a fringe
of bangs that accented dark, wide eyes. She was smiling, and the dimple was back. He wasn't sure he liked
that. When she smiled she looked as though she could
sell you ten acres of Florida swampland.

"It appears we're going to have to discuss your
cousin."

"Fred." Jackie nodded, still smiling, and slipped
onto a rattan stool at the breakfast bar. She'd already
decided she'd do best by being totally at ease and in
control. If he thought she was nervous and unsure of
her position... Well, she wasn't positive, but she had
a very good idea she'd find herself standing outside the
house, bag in hand. "He's quite a character, isn't he?
How did you meet him?"

"Through a mutual friend." He grimaced a little,
thinking he was going to have to talk with Justine, as
well. "I had a project in Germany that was going to
keep me out of the country for a few months. I needed

someone to house-sit. He was recommended. As I knew his aunt—''

"Patricia—Patricia MacNamara's my mother."

"Adele Lindstrom."

"Oh, Aunt Adele. She's my mother's sister." It was more than a smile this time. Something wickedly amused flashed in Jackie's eyes. "She's a lovely woman."

There was something droll, a bit too droll, in the comment. Nathan chose to ignore it. "I worked with Adele briefly on a revitalization project in Chicago. Because of the connection, and the recommendation, I decided to have Fred look out for the house while I was away."

Jackie bit her bottom lip. It was her first sign of nerves, and though she didn't realize it, that small gesture cleared a great deal of ground for her. "He wasn't renting it from you?"

"Renting it? Of course not." She was twisting her rings, one at a time, around her fingers. Don't get involved, he warned himself. Tell her to pack up and move out. No explanations, no apologies. You can be in bed in ten minutes. Nathan felt rather than heard his own sigh. Not many people knew that Nathan Powell was a sucker. "Is that what he told you?"

"I suppose I'd better tell you the whole story. Could I have one of those?"

When she indicated his glass, he nearly snapped at her. Manners had been bred carefully into him, and he was irritated at his oversight, even though she was hardly a guest. Without speaking, he poured and mixed another drink, then sat it in front of her. "I'd appreciate it if you could condense the whole story and just give me the highlights.''

"Okay." She took a sip, bracing herself. "Fred called me last week. He'd heard through the family grapevine that I was looking for a place to stay for a few months. A nice quiet place where I could work. I'm a writer," she said with the audacious pride of one who believed it. When this brought no response, she drank again and continued. "Anyway, Fred said he had a place that might suit me. He told me he'd been renting this house.... He described it," Jackie explained, "and I just couldn't wait to see it. It's a beautiful place, so thoughtfully designed. Now that I know who you are, I can see why—the strength and charm of the structure, the openness of the space. If I hadn't been so intent on what I was doing, I'd have recognized your style right away. I studied architecture for a couple of semesters with LaFont at Columbia."

"That's fascinating, I'm sure.... LaFont?"

"Yes, he's a wonderful old duck, isn't he? So pompous and sure of his own worth."

Nathan raised a brow. He'd studied with LaFont himself—a lifetime ago, it seemed—and was well aware that the old duck, as Jackie had termed him, only took on the most promising students. He opened his mouth again, then shut it. He wouldn't be drawn out. "Let's get back to your cousin, Miss Mac-Namara."

"Jackie," she said, flashing that smile again. "Well, if I hadn't been really anxious to get settled, I probably would have said thanks but no thanks. Fred's always got an angle. But I came down. I took one look at the place, and that was that. He said he had to leave for San Diego right away on business and that the owner—you—didn't want the house empty while you were away. I suppose you don't really just use it as a winter home sporadically, do you?''

"No." He drew a cigarette out of his pocket. He'd successfully cut down to ten a day, but these were extenuating circumstances. "I live here year-round, except when a project takes me away. The arrangement was for Fred to live here during my absence. I called two weeks ago to let him know when I'd be arriving. He was to contact Mrs. Grange and leave his forwarding address with her."

"Mrs. Grange?"

"The housekeeper."

"He didn't mention a housekeeper."

"Why doesn't that surprise me?" Nathan murmured, and finished off his drink. "That takes us to the point of your occupation."

Jackie drew a long breath. "I signed a lease. Three months. I wrote Fred a check for the rent, in advance, plus a damage deposit."

"That's unfortunate." He wouldn't feel sorry for her. He'd be damned if he would. "You didn't sign a lease with the owner."

"With your proxy. With whom I thought was your proxy," she amended. "Cousin Fred can be very smooth." He wasn't smiling, Jackie noted. Not even a glimmer. It was a pity he couldn't see the humor in the situation. "Look, Mr. Powell—Nathan—it's obvious Fred's pulled something on both of us, but there must be a way we can work it out. As far as the thirty-five hundred dollars goes—"

"Thirty-five hundred?" Nathan said. "You paid him thirty-five hundred dollars?"

"It seemed reasonable." She was tempted to pout because of his tone, but she didn't think it would help. "You do have a beautiful home, and there was the pool, and the sun room. Anyway, with a bit of family pressure, I may be able to get some of it back. Sooner or later." She thought about the money a moment longer, then dismissed it. "But the real problem is how to handle this situation."

"Which is?"

"My being here, and your being here."

"That's easy." Nathan tapped out his cigarette. There was no reason, absolutely no reason, why he should feel guilty that she'd lost money. "I can recommend a couple of excellent hotels."

She smiled again. She was sure he could, but she had no intention of going to one. The dimple was still in place, but if Nathan had looked closely he would have seen that the soft brown eyes had hardened with determination.

"That would solve your part of the problem, but not mine. I do have a lease."

"You have a worthless piece of paper."

"Very possibly." She tapped her ringed fingers on the counter as she considered. "Did you ever study law? When I was at Harvard—"

"Harvard?"

"Very briefly." She brushed away the hallowed halls with the back of her hand. "I didn't really take to it, but I do think it might be difficult and, worse, annoying to toss me out on my ear." She swirled her drink and considered. "Of course, if you wanted to get a warrant and take it to court, dragging cousin Fred into it, you'd win eventually. I'm sure of that. In the meantime," she continued before he could find the right words, "I'm sure we can come up with a much more suitable solution for everyone. You must be exhausted." She changed her tone so smoothly he could only stare. "Why don't you go on up and get a good night's sleep? Everything's clearer on a good night's sleep, don't you think? We can hash through all this tomorrow."

"It's not a matter of hashing through anything, Miss MacNamara. It's a matter of your packing up your things." He shoved a hand into his pocket, and his fingers brushed the swatch of nylon. Gritting his teeth, he pulled it out. "These are yours?"

"Yes, thanks." Without a blush, Jackie accepted her underwear. "It's a little late to be calling the cops and explaining all of this to them. I imagine you could throw me out bodily, but you'd hate yourself for it."

She had him there. Nathan began to think she had a lot more in common with her cousin than a family name. He glanced at his watch and swore. It was already after midnight, and he didn't—quite—have the heart to dump her in the street. The worst of it was that he was nearly tired enough to see double and couldn't seem to come up with the right, or the most promising, arguments. So he'd let it ride—for the moment.

"I'll give you twenty-four hours, Miss Mac-Namara. That seems more than reasonable to me."

"I knew you were a reasonable man." She smiled at him again. "Why don't you go get some sleep? I'll lock up."

"You're in my bed."

"I beg your pardon?"

"Your things are in my room."

"Oh." Jackie scratched at her temple. "Well, I suppose if it was really important to you, I could haul everything out tonight."

"Never mind." Maybe it was all a nightmare. A hallucination. He'd wake up in the morning and discover everything was as it should be. "I'll take one of the guest rooms."

"That's a much better idea. You really do look tired. Sleep well."

He stared at her for nearly a full minute. When he was gone, Jackie laid her head down on the counter and began to giggle. Oh, she'd get Fred for this, make no mistake. But now, just now, it was the funniest thing that happened to her in months.

Chapter Two

When Nathan woke, it was after ten East Coast time, but the nightmare wasn't over. He realized that as soon as he saw the muted striped paper on the wall of the guest room. He was in his own house, but he'd somehow found himself relegated to the position of guest.

His suitcases, open but still packed, sat on the mahogany chest under the garden window. He'd left his drapes undrawn, and sunlight poured in over the neatly folded shirts. Deliberately he turned away from them. He'd be damned if he'd unpack until he could do so in the privacy of his own room.

A man had a right to his own closet.

Jacqueline MacNamara had been correct about one thing. He felt better after a full night's sleep. His mind was clearer. Though it wasn't something he cared to

dwell on, he went over everything that had happened
from the time he'd unlocked his door until he'd fallen,
face first, into the guest bed.

He realized he'd been a fool not to toss her out on
her pert little ear the night before, but that could be
rectified. And the sooner the better.

He showered, taking his shaving gear into the bathroom with him, but meticulously replacing everything in the kit when he was finished. Nothing was
coming out until it could be placed in his own cabi-
nets and drawers. After he'd dressed, in light cotton
pants and shirt, he felt in charge again. If he couldn't
deal with a dippy little number like the brunette snuggled in his bed, he was definitely slipping. Still, it
wouldn't hurt to have a cup of coffee first.

He was halfway down the stairs when he smelled it.
Coffee. Strong, fresh coffee. The aroma was so welcome he nearly smiled, but then he remembered who
must have brewed it. Strengthening his resolve, he
continued. Another scent wafted toward him. Bacon? Surely that was bacon. Obviously she was making herself right at home. He heard the music, as
well—rock, something cheerful and bouncy and loud
enough to be heard a room away.

No, the nightmare wasn't over, but it was going to
end, and end quickly.

Nathan strode into the kitchen prepared to shoot
straight from the hip.

"Good morning." Jackie greeted him with a smile
that competed with the sunshine. As a concession to
him, she turned the radio down, but not off. "I wasn't
sure how long you'd sleep, but I didn't think you were
the type to stay in bed through the morning, so I

started breakfast. I hope you like blueberry pancakes. I slipped out early and bought the berries. They're fresh." Before he could speak, she popped one into his mouth. "Have a seat. I'll get your coffee."

"Miss MacNamara—"

"Jackie, please. Cream?"

"Black. We left things a bit up in the air last night, but we've got to settle this business now."

"Absolutely. I hope you like your bacon crisp." She set a platter on the counter, where a place was already set with his good china and a damask napkin. She noticed that he'd shaved. With the shadow of beard gone, he didn't look quite as much like her Jake—except around the eyes. It wouldn't be wise, she decided, to underestimate him.

"I've given it a lot of thought, Nathan, and I think I've come up with the ideal solution." She poured batter onto the griddle and adjusted the flame. "Did you sleep well?"

"Fine." At least he'd felt fine when he'd awakened. Now he reached for the coffee almost defensively. She was like a sunbeam that had intruded when all he'd really wanted to do was draw the shades and take a nap.

"My mother's fond of saying you always sleep best at home, but it's never mattered to me. I can sleep anywhere. Would you like the paper?"

"No." He sipped the coffee, stared at it, then sipped again. Maybe it was his imagination, but it was the best cup of coffee he'd ever tasted.

"I buy the beans from a little shop in town," she said, answering his unspoken question as she flipped the pancakes with an expert hand. "I don't drink it often myself. That's why I think it's important to have a really good cup. Ready for these?" Before he could answer, she took his plate and stacked pancakes on it. "You've a wonderful view from right here." Jackie poured a second cup of coffee and sat beside him. "It makes eating an event."

Nathan found himself reaching for the syrup. It wouldn't hurt to eat first. He could still toss her out later. "How long have you been here?"

"Just a few days. Fred's always had an excellent sense of timing. How are your pancakes?"

It seemed only fair to give her her due. "They're wonderful. Aren't you eating?"

"I sort of sampled as I went along." But that didn't stop her from plucking another slice of bacon. She nibbled, approved, then smiled at him. "Do you cook?"

"Only if the package comes with instructions."

Jackie felt the first thrill of victory. "I'm really a very good cook."

"Studied at the Cordon Bleu, I imagine."

"Only for six months," she said, grinning at him. "But I did learn most of the basics. From there I decided to go my own way, experiment, you know? Cooking should be as much of an adventure as anything else."

To Nathan, cooking was drudgery that usually ended in failure. He only grunted.

"Your Mrs. Grange," Jackie began conversationally. "Is she supposed to come in every day, do the cleaning and the cooking?"

"Once a week." The pancakes were absolutely fabulous. He'd grown accustomed to hotel food, and as excellent as it had been, it couldn't compete with this. He began to relax as he studied the view. She was right, it was great, and he couldn't remember ever having enjoyed breakfast more. "She cleans, does the weekly marketing, and usually fixes a casserole or something." Nathan took another forkful, then stopped himself before he could again be seduced by the flavor. "Why?"

"It all has to do with our little dilemma."

"Your dilemma."

"Whatever. I wonder, are you a fair man, Nathan? Your buildings certainly show a sense of style and order, but I can't really tell if you have a sense of fair play." She lifted the coffeepot. "Let me top that off for you."

He was losing his appetite rapidly. "What are you getting at?"

"I'm out thirty-five hundred." Jackie munched on the bacon. "Now, I'm not going to try to make you think that the loss is going to have me on the street-corner selling pencils, but it's not really the amount. It's the principle. You believe in principles, don't you?"

Cautious, he gave a noncommittal shrug.

"I paid, in good faith, for a place to live and to work for three months."

"I'm sure your family retains excellent lawyers. Why don't you sue your cousin?"

"The MacNamaras don't solve family problems that way. Oh, I'll settle up with him—when he least expects it."

There was a look in her eyes that made Nathan think she would do just that, and beautifully. He had to fight back a surge of admiration. "I'll wish you the best of luck here, but your family problems don't involve me."

"They do when it's your house in the middle of it. Do you want some more?"

"No. Thanks," he added belatedly. "Miss— Jackie—I'm going to be perfectly frank with you." He settled back, prepared to be both reasonable and firm. If he'd known her better, Nathan would have felt his first qualms when she turned her big brown eyes on him with a look of complete cooperation. "My work in Germany was difficult and tiring. I have a couple of months of free time coming, which I intend to spend here, alone, doing as little as possible."

"What were you building?"

"What?"

"In Germany. What were you building?"

"An entertainment complex, but that isn't really relevant. I'm sorry if it seems insensitive, but I don't feel responsible for your situation."

"It doesn't seem insensitive at all." Jackie patted his hand, then poured him more coffee. "Why should you, after all? An entertainment complex. It sounds fascinating, and I'd really love to hear all about it later, but the thing is, Nathan—" she paused as she topped off her own cup "—is that I kind of see us as two people in the same boat. We both expected to spend the next couple of months alone, pursuing our own projects, and Fred screwed up the works. Do you like Oriental food?"

He was losing ground. Nathan didn't know why, or when, the sand had started to shift beneath his feet, but there it was. Resting his elbows on the counter, he held his head in his hands. "What the hell does that have to do with anything?"

"It has to do with my idea, and I wanted to know what kind of food you liked, or particularly didn't like. Me, I'll eat anything, but most people have definite preferences." Jackie cupped her mug in both hands as she tucked her legs, lotus-style, under her on the stool. She was wearing shorts today, vivid blue ones with a flamingo emblem on one leg. Nathan studied the odd pink bird for a long time before he lifted his gaze to hers.

"Why don't you just tell me your idea while I still have a small part of my sanity?"

"The object is for both of us to have what we want—or as nearly as possible. It's a big house."

She lifted both brows as his eyes narrowed. That look, she thought again. That Jake look was hard to resist. Nathan's coming back when he did might have been the sort of odd bonus fate sometimes tossed out. Jackie was always ready to make the grab for it.

"I'm an excellent roommate. I could give you references from several people. I went to a variety of colleges, you see, so I lived with a variety of people. I can be neat if that's important, and I can be quiet and unobtrusive."

"I find that difficult to believe."

"No, really, especially when I'm immersed in my own project, like I am now. I write almost all day. This story's really the most important thing in my life right now. I'll have to tell you about it, but we'll save that."

"I'd appreciate it."

"You have a wonderfully subtle sense of humor, Nathan. Don't ever lose it. Anyhow, I'm a strong believer in atmosphere. You must be, too, being an architect."

"You're losing me again." He shoved the coffee aside. Too much stimulation, that must be it. Another cup and he might just start understanding her.

"The house," Jackie said patiently. Her eyes were the problem, Nathan decided. There was something about them that compelled you to look and listen when all you really wanted to do was hold your hands over your ears and run.

"What about the house?"

"There's something about it. The minute I set up here, everything just started flowing. With the story. If I moved, well, don't you think things might stop flowing just as quickly? I don't want to chance that. So I'm willing to make some compromises."

"You're willing to make some compromises," Nathan repeated slowly. "That's fascinating. You're living in my house, without my consent, but you're willing to make some compromises."

"It's only fair." There was that smile again, quick and brilliant. "You don't cook. I do." Jackie gestured with both hands as if to show the simplicity of it. "I'll prepare all of your meals, at my expense, for as long as I'm here."

It sounded reasonable. Why in the hell did it sound so reasonable when she said it? "That's very generous of you, but I don't want a cook, or a roommate."

"How do you know? You haven't had either yet."

"What I want," he began, careful to space his words and keep his tone even, "is privacy."

"Of course you do." She didn't touch him, but her tone was like a pat on the head. He nearly growled. "We'll make a pact right now. I'll respect your privacy and you'll respect mine. Nathan . . ." She leaned toward him, again covering his hand with hers in a move that was natural rather than calculated. "I know you've got absolutely no reason to do me any favors, but I'm really committed to this book. For reasons of my own, I've a great need to finish it, and I'm sure I can. Here."

"If you're trying to make me feel guilty because I'd be sabotaging the great American novel—"

"No, I'm not. I would have if I'd thought of it, but I didn't. I'm just asking you to give me a chance. A couple of weeks. If I drive you crazy, I'll leave."

"Jacqueline, I've known you about twelve hours, and you've already driven me crazy."

She was winning. There was just the slightest hint of it in his tone, but she caught it and pounced. "You ate all your pancakes."

Almost guiltily, Nathan looked down at his empty plate. "I've had nothing but airplane food for twenty-four hours."

"Wait until you taste my crepes. And my Belgian waffles." She caught her lower lip between her teeth. "Nathan, think of it. You won't have to open a single can as long as I'm around."

Involuntarily he thought of all the haphazard meals he'd prepared, and about the barely edible ones he brought into the house in Styrofoam containers. "I'll eat out."

"A fat lot of privacy you'd have sitting in crowded restaurants and competing for a waiter's attention. With my solution, you won't have to do anything but relax."

He hated restaurants. And God knew he'd had enough of them over the past year. The arrangement made perfect sense, at least while he was comfortably full of her blueberry pancakes.

"I want my room back."

"That goes without saying."

"And I don't like small talk in the morning."

"Completely uncivilized. I do want pool privileges."

"If I stumble over you or any of your things even once, you're out."

"Agreed." She held out a hand, sensing he was a man who would stand by a handshake. She was even more certain of it when she saw him hesitate. Jackie brought out what she hoped would be the coup de grace. "You really would hate yourself if you threw me out, you know."

Nathan scowled at her but found his palm resting against hers. A small hand, and a soft one, he thought, but the grip was firm. If he lived to regret this temporary arrangement, he'd have one more score to settle with Fred. "I'm going to take a spa."

"Good idea. Loosen up all those tense muscles. By the way, what would you like for lunch?"

He didn't look back. "Surprise me."

Jackie picked up his plate and did a quick dance around the kitchen.

* * *

Temporary insanity. Nathan debated the wisdom of pleading that cause to his associates, his family or the higher courts. He had a boarder. A nonpaying one at that. Nathan Powell, a conservative, upstanding member of society, a member of the Fortune 500, the thirty-two-year-old wunderkind of architecture, had a strange woman in his house.

He didn't necessarily mean strange as in unknown. Jackie MacNamara *was* strange. He'd come to that conclusion when he'd seen her meditating by the pool after lunch. He'd glanced out and spotted her, sitting cross-legged on the stone apron, head tilted back, eyes closed, hands resting lightly on her knees, palms up. He'd been mortally afraid she was reciting a mantra. Did people still do that sort of thing?

He must have been insane to agree to her arrangement because of blueberry pancakes and a smile. Jet lag, he decided as he poured another glass of iced tea Jackie had made to go with a truly exceptional spinach salad. Even a competent, intelligent man could fall victim to the weakness of the body after a transatlantic flight.

Two weeks, he reminded himself. Technically, he'd only agreed to two weeks. After that time had passed, he could gently but firmly ease her on her way. In the meantime, he would do what he should have done hours ago—make certain he didn't have a maniac on his hands.

There was a neat leather-bound address book by the kitchen phone, as there was by every phone in the house. Nathan flipped through it to the *L*'s. Jackie was upstairs working on her book—if indeed there was a book at all. He would make the call, glean a few pertinent facts, then decide how to move from there.

"Lindstrom residence."

"Adele Lindstrom, please, Nathan Powell calling."

"One moment, Mr. Powell."

Nathan sipped tea as he waited. A man could become addicted to having it made fresh instead of digging crystallized chemicals out of a jar. Absently he drew a cigarette out of his pocket and tapped the filter on the counter.

"Nathan, dear, how are you?"

"Adele. I'm very well, and you?"

"Couldn't be better, though March insists on going out like a lion here. What can I do for you, dear? Are you in Chicago?"

"No, actually I've just arrived home. Your nephew Fred was, ah...house-sitting for me."

"Of course, I remember." There was a long, and to Nathan pregnant, pause. "Fred hasn't done something naughty, has he?"

Naughty? Nathan passed a hand over his face. After a moment, he decided not to blast Adele with the sad facts of the situation, but to tone it down. "We do have a bit of a mix-up. Your niece is here."

"Niece? Well, I have several of those. Jacqueline? Of course it's Jacqueline. I remember now that Honoria—that's Fred's mother—told me that little Jack was going south. Poor Nathan, you've a houseful of MacNamaras."

"Actually, Fred's in San Diego."

"San Diego? What are you all doing in San Diego?"

Nathan tried to remember if Adele Lindstrom had been quite this scattered in Chicago. "Fred's in San Diego—at least I think he is. I'm in Florida, with your niece."

"Oh... Oh!" The second *oh* had enough delight in it to put Nathan on guard. "Well, isn't that lovely? I've always said that all our Jacqueline needed was a nice, stable man. She's a bit of a butterfly, of course, but very bright and wonderfully good-hearted."

"I'm sure she is." Nathan found it necessary to put the record straight, and to put it straight quickly. "She's only here because of a misunderstanding. It seems Fred...didn't understand that I was coming back, and he...offered the house to Jackie."

"I see." And she did, perfectly. Fortunately for Nathan, he couldn't see her eyes light with amusement. "How awkward for you. I hope you and Jacqueline have worked things out."

"More or less. You're her mother's sister?"

"That's right. Jackie favors Patricia physically. Such a piquant look. I was always jealous as a child. Otherwise, none of us have ever been quite sure who little Jackie takes after."

Nathan blew out a stream of smoke. "That doesn't surprise me."

"What is it now...painting? No, it's writing. Jackie's a novelist these days."

"So she says."

"I'm sure she'll tell a delightful story. She's always been full of them."

"I'll just bet."

"Well, dear, I know the two of you will get along fine. Our little Jack manages to get along with just about anyone. A talent of hers. Not to say that Patricia and I hadn't hoped she'd be settled down and married by now—put some of that energy into raising a nice family. She's a sweet girl—a bit flighty, but sweet. You're still single, aren't you, Nathan?''

With his eyes cast up to the ceiling, he shook his head. "Yes, I am. It's been nice talking to you, Adele. I'll suggest to your niece that she get in touch when she relocates.''

"That would be nice. It's always a pleasure to hear from Jack. And you, too, Nathan. Be sure to let me know if you get to Chicago again.''

"I will. Take care of yourself, Adele.''

He hung up, still frowning at the phone. There was little doubt that his unwanted tenant was exactly who she said she was. But that didn't really accomplish anything. He could talk to her again, but when he'd tried to do that over lunch, he'd gotten a small, and very nagging, headache. It might be the coward's way, but for the rest of the day he was going to pretend that Jacqueline MacNamara, with her long legs and her brilliant smile, didn't exist.

Upstairs, in front of her typewriter, Jackie wasn't giving Nathan a thought. Or if she was she'd twined him so completely with the hard-bitten and heroic Jake that she wasn't able to see the difference.

It was working. Sometimes, when her fingers slowed just a bit and her mind whipped back to the present, she was struck by the wonderful and delightful thought that she was really writing. Not playing at it, as she had played at so many other things.

She knew her family tut-tutted about her. All those brains and all that breeding, and Jackie could never seem to make up her mind what to do with them. She was happy to announce that this time she had found something, and that it had found her.

Sitting back, her tongue caught between her teeth, she read the last scene over. It was good, she was sure of that. She knew that back in Newport there were those who would shake their heads and smile indulgently. So what if the scene was good, or even if several chapters were good? Dear little Jack never finished anything.

In her stint at remodeling, she'd bought a huge rat-trap of a house and had scraped, planed, painted and papered. She'd learned about plumbing and rewiring, had haunted lumberyards and hardware stores. The first floor—she'd always believed in starting from the bottom up—had been fabulous. She was creative and competent. The problem had been, as it always had been, that once the first rush of excitement was over something else had caught her interest. The house had lost its charm for her. True, she'd sold it at a nice profit, but she'd never touched the two upper stories.

This was different.

Jackie cradled her chin in her hand. How many times had she said that before? The photography studio, the dance classes, the potter's wheel. But this *was* different. She'd been fascinated by each field she'd tampered in, and in each had shown a nice ability to apply what she'd learned, but she was beginning to see, or hope, that all those experiments, all those false starts, had been leading up to this.

She had to be right about the story. This time she had to carry it through from start to finish. Nothing else she'd tried had been so important or seemed so right. It didn't matter that her family and friends saw her as eccentric and fickle. She *was* eccentric and fickle. But there had to be something, something strong and meaningful, in her life. She couldn't go on playing at being an adult forever.

The great American novel. That made her smile. No, it wouldn't be that. In fact, Jackie couldn't think of many things more tedious than attempting to write the great American novel. But it could be a good book, a book people might care about and enjoy, one they might curl up with on a quiet evening. That would be enough. She hadn't realized that before, but once she'd really begun to care about it herself she'd known that would be more than enough.

It was coming so fast, almost faster than she could handle. The room was stacked with reference books and manuals, writers' how-tos and guides. She'd pored over them all. Researching her subject was the one discipline Jackie had always followed strictly. She'd been grateful for the road maps, the explanations of pitfalls and the suggestions. Oddly, now that she was hip deep in the story, none of that seemed to matter. She was writing on instinct and by the seat of her pants. As far as she could remember—and her memory was keen—she'd never had more fun in her life.

She closed her eyes to think about Jake. Instantly her mind took a leap to Nathan. Wasn't it strange how much he looked like her own conception of the hero of her story? It really did make it all seem fated. Jackie had a healthy respect for fate, particularly after her study of astrology.

Not that Nathan was a reckless gunslinger. No, he was rather sweetly conservative. A man, she was sure, who thought of himself as organized and practical. She doubted seriously that he considered himself an artist, though he was undoubtedly a talented one. He'd also be a list-maker and a plan-follower. She respected that, though she'd never been able to stick with a list in her life. What she admired even more was that he was a man who knew what he wanted and had accomplished it.

He was also a pleasure to look at—particularly when he smiled. The smile was usually reluctant, which made it all the sweeter. Already she'd decided it was her duty to nudge that smile from him as often as possible.

It shouldn't be difficult. Obviously he had a good heart; otherwise he would have given her the heave-ho the first night. That he hadn't, though he'd certainly wanted to, made Jackie think rather kindly of him. Because she did, she was determined to make their cohabitation as painless for him as possible.

She didn't doubt that they could deal very nicely with each other for a few months. In truth, she preferred company, even his reluctant sort, to solitude.

She liked his subtlety, and his well-bred sarcasm. Even someone much less sensitive than she would have recognized the fact that nothing would have made him happier than to dispose of her. It was a pity she couldn't oblige him, but she really was determined to finish her book, and to finish it where she had started it.

While she was at it, she'd stay out of his way as much as was humanly possible, and fix him some of the best meals of his life.

That thought made her glance at her watch. She swore a little, but turned off her machine. It really was a pain to have to think about dinner when Jake was tethered by a leather thong to the wrist of an Apache brave. The knife fight was just heating up; but a bargain was a bargain.

Humming to herself, she started down to the kitchen.

Once again it was the scents that lured him. Nathan had been perfectly happy catching up on his back issues of Architectural Digest. He burrowed in his office, content simply to be there with the warm paneled walls and the faded Persian carpet. Terrace doors opened onto the patio and out to the garden. It was his refuge, with the faint scent of leather from books and the sharp light of sun through etched glass. If a man couldn't be alone in his office, he couldn't be alone anywhere.

Late in the afternoon he'd nearly been able to erase Jackie MacNamara and her conniving cousin from his mind. He'd heard her humming, and had ignored it. That had pleased him. A servant. He would think of her as a servant and nothing more.

Then the aromas had started teasing him. Hot, spicy aromas. She was playing the radio again. Loud. He really was going to have to speak to her about that. Nathan shifted in his office chair and tried to concentrate.

Was that chicken? he wondered, and lost his place in an article on earth homes. He thought about closing the door, flipped a page and found the Top 40 number Jackie was playing at top volume juggling around in his head. Telling himself she needed a lecture on music appreciation, he set the magazine aside—after marking his place—then headed toward the kitchen.

He had to speak to her twice before she heard him. Jackie kept a hand on the handle of the frying pan, shaking it gently as she pitched her voice to a shout.

"It'll be ready in a few minutes. Would you like some wine?"

"No. What I'd like is for you to turn that thing off."

"To what?"

"To turn that thing—" Almost growling in disgust, Nathan walked over to the kitchen speaker and hit the switch. "Haven't you ever heard about inner-ear damage?"

Jackie gave the pan another shake before turning off the flame. "I always play the music loud when I'm cooking. It inspires me."

"Invest in headphones," he suggested.

With a shrug, Jackie took the lid off the rice and gave it a quick swipe with a fork. "Sorry. I figured since you had speakers in every room you liked music. How was your day? Did you get plenty of rest?"

Something in her tone made him feel like a cranky grandfather. "I'm fine," he said between his teeth.

"Good. I hope you like Chinese. I have a friend who owns a really wonderful little Oriental restaurant in San Francisco. I persuaded his chef to share some recipes." Jackie poured Nathan a glass of wine. She was using his Waterford this time. In the smooth and economical way she had in the kitchen, she scooped the sweet-and-sour chicken onto a bed of rice. "I didn't have time for fortune cookies, but there's an upside-down cake in the oven." She licked sauce from her thumb before she began to serve herself. "You don't want to let that get cold."

Wary of her, he sat. A man had to eat, after all. As he forked a cube of chicken, he watched her. Nothing seemed to break her rhythm, or her breezy sense of self-confidence. He'd see about that, Nathan thought, and waited until she'd joined him at the bar.

"I spoke with your aunt today."

"Really? Aunt Adele?" Jackie hooked one bare foot around the leg of the stool. "Did she give me a good reference?"

"More or less."

"You brought it on yourself," she said, then began to eat with the steady enthusiasm of one who liked food for food's sake.

"I beg your pardon?"

Jackie sampled a bamboo shoot. "Word's going to spread like wildfire, through the Lindstrom branch and over to the MacNamaras. I imagine it'll detour through the O'Brians too. That's my father's sister's married name." She took a forkful of saffron rice. "I can't take the responsibility."

Now it was he who'd lost his rhythm. Again. "I don't know what you're talking about."

"The wedding."

"What wedding?"

"Ours." She picked up her glass and sipped, smiling at him over the rim. "What do you think of the wine?"

"Back up. What do you mean, our wedding?"

"Well, I don't mean it, and you don't mean it. But Aunt Adele will mean it. Twenty minutes after you spoke with her she'd have been chirping happily about our romance to anyone who'd listen. People do listen to Aunt Adele. I've never understood why. You're letting that chicken get cold, Nathan."

He set his fork down, keeping his voice even and his eyes steady. "I never gave her any reason to think we were involved."

"Of course you didn't." Obviously on his side, Jackie squeezed his arm. "All you did was tell Aunt Adele I was living here." The timer buzzed, so Jackie scooted up to pull the cake out of the oven. Wanting a moment to think, Nathan waited until she'd set it out to cool and joined him again.

"I explained there'd been a misunderstanding."

"She has a very selective memory." Jackie took another generous bite. "Don't worry, I won't hold you to it. Do you think there's enough ginger in this?"

"There's nothing to hold me to."

"Not between us." She sent him a sympathetic glance. "Don't let it ruin your appetite. I can handle the family. Can I ask you a personal question?"

Nathan picked up his fork again. Somehow he'd opened the door to his own house and fallen down the rabbit hole. "Why not?"

"Are you involved with anyone? It doesn't have to be particularly serious."

She liked the way his eyes narrowed. There was something about gray eyes, really gray eyes, that could cut right through you.

He debated half a dozen answers before settling on the truth. "No."

"That's too bad." Her forehead wrinkled briefly before smoothing out again. "It would have helped if you were, but I'll just make something up. Would you mind very much if I threw you over, maybe for a marine biologist?"

He was laughing. He didn't know why, but when he reached for his wine, his lips were still curved. "Not at all."

She hadn't counted on that—that his laugh would be so appealing. The little flutter came. Jackie acknowledged it, savored it briefly, then banked it down. It wouldn't do. No, it wouldn't do at all. "You're a good sport, Nathan. Not everyone would think so, but they don't know you like I do. Let me get you some more chicken."

"No, I'll get it."

It was a small mistake, the kind people make every day when they step into a doorway at the same time or bump elbows in a crowded elevator. The kind of small mistake that is rarely recognized and soon forgotten.

They rose simultaneously, both reaching for his plate. Their hands closed over it, and each other's. Their bodies bumped. He took her arm to steady her. The usual quick smile and the automatic apology didn't come from either of them.

Jackie felt her breath snag and her heart stumble. The feeling didn't surprise her. She was too much in tune with her emotions, too comfortable with them, to be surprised. It was the depth of them that caught at her. The contact was casual, more funny than romantic, but she felt as though she'd been waiting all her life for it.

She'd remember the feel of his hand, and the china, and the heat of his body as it barely brushed hers. She'd remember the look of surprised suspicion in his eyes, and the scent of spices and wine. She'd remember the quiet, the absolute and sudden quiet. As if the world had held its breath for a moment. For just a moment.

What the hell was this? That was his first and only coherent thought. He was gripping her harder than he should have, as if he were holding on—but that was absurd. However absurd it was, he couldn't quite make himself let go. Her eyes were so big, so soft. Was it foolish to believe he saw absolute honesty in them? That scent, her scent, was there, the one he'd first come across in his own bedroom. The one, Nathan thought now, that still lingered, ridiculously, after she'd moved into a guest room. He heard her breath suck in, then shudder out. Or maybe it was his own.

And he wanted her, as clearly and as logically as he'd ever wanted anything. It lasted only a moment, but the desire was strong.

They moved away together, with the quick, almost jerky motion one uses when one steps back from an unexpected flame. Jackie cleared her throat. Nathan let out a long, quiet breath.

"It's no trouble," she said.

"Thanks."

She moved to the stove before she thought she could breathe easily. As she scooped up chicken and vegetables, she wondered if this was one adventure she should have passed on.

Chapter Three

When he looked at her something happened, something frantic, something she'd never experienced before. Her heart beat just a little too fast, and dampness sprang out on the palms of her hands. A look was all that was necessary. His eyes were so dark, so penetrating. When he looked at her it was as if he could see everything she was, or could be, or wanted to be.

It was absurd. He was a man who lived by the gun, who took what he wanted without regret or compassion. All of her life she'd been taught that the line between right and wrong was clear and wide, and couldn't be crossed.

To kill was the greatest sin, the most unforgivable. Yet he had killed, and would surely kill again. Knowing it, she couldn't care for him. But care she did. And want she did. And need.

Sitting back, Jackie reviewed Sarah's confused and contrasting feelings for Jake. How would a sheltered young woman, barely eighteen, respond to a man who had lived all his life by rules she couldn't possibly understand or approve of? And how would a man who had seen and done all that Jake Redman had seen and done react to an innocent, convent-bred woman?

There was no way their dealings with each other could run smoothly. Their coming together and its resolution couldn't be impossible, it just had to be difficult. Two different worlds, she thought. Two sets of values, two opposing ambitions. Those would be difficult conflicts to overcome. Then you added gunfights, betrayal, kidnapping and revenge. Just to keep things interesting. Still, for all the action and adventure, Jackie had come to think that the love story was really the heart of her book. How these two people were going to change and complement each other, how they would compromise, adjust and stand firm.

She didn't think Sarah or Jake would understand about emotional commitment or mutually supportive relationships. Those were twentieth-century terms. Her psychology course on modern marriage had given Jackie a basketful of catchphrases. The words might change, but love was love. As far as she was concerned, Sarah and Jake had a good chance. That was more than a great many people could say.

It occurred to her that that was all she wanted for herself. A good chance. Someone to love who would love her back, someone to make adjustments for, to make long-range plans with. Wasn't it strange that in making a relationship on paper she had begun to fantasize about making one for herself?

She wouldn't ask for perfection, not only because it would be boring but because she would never be able to achieve perfection herself. It wouldn't be necessary, or even appealing, to settle down with a man who agreed with you on every point.

Would she like dashing? Probably. It might be fun to have someone flash in and out of your life, dropping off dew-kissed roses and magnums of champagne. It would be a nice interlude, but she was dead certain she couldn't live with dashing. Dashing would never take out the trash or unclog a drain.

Sensitive. Jackie rolled the word around in her mind, coming up with a picture of a sweet, caring man who wrote bad poetry. Horn-rimmed glasses and a voice like cream. Sensitive would always understand a woman's needs and a woman's moods. She could be very fond of sensitive. Until sensitive began to drive her crazy.

Passionate would be nice, as well. Someone who would toss her over his shoulder and make mad love in sun-drenched fields. But it might get a bit tough to do that sort of thing once they hit eighty.

Funny, intelligent, reckless and dependable.

That was the trouble, she supposed. She could think of a dozen different qualities she would enjoy in a man, but not of a combination that would pull her in for the long haul. With a sigh, she cupped her chin in her hand and stared over the typewriter through the window. Maybe she just wasn't ready to think about wedding rings and picket fences. Maybe she'd never be ready.

It wasn't easy to accept, but if it was true she could see herself living in some quaint little house near the water and writing about other people's love affairs. She could spend her days dreaming up characters and places, puttering around in a garden and playing aunt to all the little MacNamaras. It wouldn't be so bad.

She wouldn't be a hermit, of course. And it wasn't as though she didn't appreciate men. Any man she'd ever been close to had possessed at least one of the qualities she admired. She'd cared for and about them, even loved them a little. But then, love was easy for her, falling in and falling out of it without bruises or scars. That wasn't real romance, she thought as she looked at the words she'd written. Real romance scraped off a little skin. It had to if love was going to bloom out of it and heal.

Lord, she was getting philosophical since she'd started putting words on paper. Maybe that explained her reaction to Nathan.

The problem was, though she was clever with words and always had been, she couldn't quite come up with the right ones to describe that one brief moment of contact.

Intense, confusing, illuminating, scary. It had been all of those, yet she wasn't sure what the sum of the parts equaled.

Attraction, certainly. But then, she'd found him attractive even when she'd thought she was hallucinating. Most women found dark, brooding types with aloof qualities attractive. God knew why. Yet that one moment, that quick link, had been more than simple attraction. The fact was, it hadn't been simple anything. She'd wanted him in the strong, vital way that usually came only with understanding and time.

I know you, something had seemed to say inside her. And I've been waiting.

He'd felt something too. She was certain of that. Maybe it had been that same kind of instant knowledge and instant desire. Whatever he'd felt hadn't pleased him, because he'd been very careful to avoid her for the better part of two days. Not an easy trick, since they were living in the same house, but he'd managed.

She still thought it had been rather rude of him to go out on his boat for an entire day and not ask her along.

Maybe he had to think things through. Jackie gauged him as the type of man who would have to compute and analyze and reason out every area of his life, including the emotional. That was too bad, but she'd have been the first to say that everyone was entitled to their own quirks.

He didn't have to worry about her, she decided as she dipped into a bowl of cheese curls. She wasn't interested in flirting with a relationship, and certainly not one with a man as buttoned-down as Nathan Powell. If she were, then he'd have reason to worry. Jackie chuckled to herself as she nibbled. She could be very tenacious and very persuasive when her mind was set. Fortunately for him, and perhaps for both of them, she was much too involved with writing to give him more than a passing thought.

Still, she checked her watch and noticed that it was nearly dinnertime and he wasn't back. His problem, she thought as she took another handful of cheese curls. She'd agreed to cook, but not to cater. When he came home he could make himself a sandwich. It certainly didn't matter to her.

She peered out her window at the sound of a boat, then settled back with the smallest of sighs when it passed by.

She wasn't really thinking of him, she told herself. She was just...passing the time. She didn't really wish he'd asked her to join him today so that they could have spent some time alone together, getting to know each other better. She wasn't really wondering what kind of man he was—except in the most intellectual terms.

What did it matter that she liked the way he laughed when he briefly let his guard down? It certainly wasn't important that his eyes were dark and dangerous one minute and quietly sensitive another. He was just a man, bound up in his work and his self-image in the same way she was bound up in her work and her future. It wasn't any of her business that he seemed more tense than he should be, and more solitary. It wasn't her goal in life to draw him out and urge him to relax and enjoy.

Her goal in life, Jackie reminded herself, was to finish the story, sell it and reap the benefits of being a published novelist. Whatever they might be. Straightening in her seat, she pushed Nathan Powell aside and went back to work.

This was what he'd come home for, Nathan told himself as he cruised down one of the narrow, deserted channels. Peace and quiet. There were no deadlines, no contract dates to worry about, no supply shortages to work around or inspectors to answer to. Sun and water. He didn't want to think beyond them.

He was beginning to feel almost like himself again. It was odd that he hadn't thought of this before—taking the boat out and disappearing for the day. He might have agreed to have a boarder for a couple of weeks, but that didn't mean he had to chain himself to the house. Or to her.

He couldn't say that it was entirely unpleasant having her there. She was keeping her end of the bargain. Most days passed without him seeing her at all except in the kitchen. Somehow he'd even gotten used to hearing her pounding away at the keys of her typewriter for hours on end. She might have been writing nursery rhymes for all he knew, but he couldn't say she wasn't keeping at it.

Actually, there were a lot of things he couldn't say about her. The problem started with the things he could say.

She talked too fast. It might have seemed an odd complaint, but not for a man who preferred quiet and structured conversations. If they talked about the weather she'd mention her brief career as a meterologist and end by saying she liked rain because it smelled nice. Who could keep up with that sort of thought pattern?

She anticipated him. He might just begin to think he could use a cold drink and he'd find her in the kitchen making iced tea or pouring him a beer. Though she hadn't yet indicated that she'd trained as a psychic, he found it disconcerting.

She always looked at ease. It was a difficult thing to fault her for, but he found himself growing tenser the more casual she became. Invariably she was dressed in shorts and some breezy top with no makeup and her hair curling as it chose. She stopped just short of being sloppy, and he shouldn't have found it alluring. He preferred well-groomed, polished women—women with a little gloss and style. So why couldn't he keep his mind off one coltish, unpainted throwback who didn't do anything more to attract him than scrub her face and grin?

Because she was different? Nathan could easily reject that notion. He was a man who preferred the comfortable, and the comfortable usually meant the familiar. There was certainly nothing remotely familiar about Jackie. Some might accuse him of being in a rut, but he thought himself entitled. When your career took you to different cities and different countries and involved different people and problems on a regular basis, you deserved a nice comfortable rut in your personal life.

Solitude, quiet, a good book, an occasional congenial companion over drinks or dinner. It didn't seem like too much to ask. Jacqueline MacNamara had thrown a wrench in the works.

He didn't like to admit it, but he was getting used to her. After only a few days, he was used to her company. That in itself, for a loner, was a shattering discovery.

Nathan opened the throttle to let his boat race. He might have been more comfortable if she'd been dull or drab. For social purposes he preferred refined and composed, but for a housemate—boarder, he reminded himself firmly—for a boarder he'd have been happy with dull.

The trouble was, no matter how quiet or unobtrusive she was for most of the day, she was impossible to ignore with her rapid-fire conversations, her dazzling smiles and her bright clothes. Especially since she never seemed to dress in anything that covered more than ten percent of her.

Maybe he could admit it now, alone, with the wind breezing through his hair and over his face, that as annoying and inconvenient as it was to have his sanctuary invaded, she was, well . . . fun.

He hadn't allowed himself a great deal of fun in the past few years. Work had been and still was his first priority. Building, the creative process and the actual nuts and bolts, absorbed his time. He'd never resented the responsibility. If anyone had asked him if he enjoyed his work, he would have given them a peculiar look and answered, "Of course." Why else would he do it?

He would have accepted the term *dedicated* but would have knit his brows at the word *obsessed*, though obsessed was exactly what he was. He could picture a building in his mind, complete, down to the smallest detail, but he didn't consider himself an artist when he drew up the blueprints. He was a professional, educated and trained, nothing more or less.

He loved his work and considered himself lucky to have found a profession for which he had both skill and affection. There were moments of sweaty, gritty work, head-throbbing concentration and absolute pride. Nothing, absolutely nothing, had ever given him the same thrill of accomplishment as seeing one of his buildings completed.

If he absorbed himself in his work, it wasn't that his life was lacking in other areas. It was simply that no other area had the same appeal or excitement for him. He enjoyed the company of women, but had never met one who could keep him awake at night the way an engineering problem with a building could.

Unless, of course, he counted Jackie. He didn't care to.

He squinted into the sun, then steered away from it until it spread its warmth across his back. Still his frown remained.

Her conversations were like puzzles he had to sort out. No one had made him think that intricately in years. Her constant cheerfulness was contagious. It would be foolish to deny he hadn't eaten better since his childhood—and probably not even then.

She did have an affecting smile, he thought as he wound his way down an alley of the waterway. And her eyes were so big and dark. Dark, yes, but they had this trick, this illusion of lighting up when she smiled. And her mouth was so wide and so generous, always ready to curve.

Nathan pulled himself up short. Her physical attributes weren't of any consequence. Shouldn't be.

That one moment of connection had been a fluke. And he was undoubtedly exaggerating the depth of it. There might have been a passing attraction. That was natural enough. But there certainly hadn't been the affinity he'd imagined. He didn't believe in such things. Love at first sight was a convenience used by novelists—usually bad ones. And instant desire was only lust given a prettier name.

Whatever he had felt, if he'd felt anything at all, had been a vague and temporary tug, purely physical and easily subdued.

Nathan could almost hear her laughing at him, though he was alone on the water and the banks of the waterway were almost deserted. Grimly he headed home.

It was dusk when she heard his boat. Jackie was certain it was Nathan. For the past two hours her ears had been fine-tuned for his return. The wave of relief came first. He hadn't met with any of the hideous boating accidents her mind had conjured up for him. Nor had he been kidnapped and held for ransom. He was back, safe and sound. She wanted to punch him right in the mouth.

Twelve hours, she thought as she dived cleanly into the pool. He'd been gone for nearly twelve hours. The man obviously had no sense of consideration.

Naturally, she hadn't been worried. She'd been much too busy with her own projects to give him more than a passing thought—every five minutes for the last two hours.

Jackie began to do laps in a steady freestyle to release her pent-up energy. She wasn't angry. Why, she wasn't even mildly annoyed. His life was most certainly his own, to do with exactly as he chose. She wouldn't say a word about it. Not a word.

She did twenty laps, then tossed her wet hair back before resting her elbows on the edge of the pool.

"Training for the Olympics?" Nathan asked her. He stood only a few feet away, a glass of clear, fizzing liquid in his hand. Jackie blinked water out of her eyes and frowned at him.

He was wearing shorts, pleated and pressed, and a short-sleeved polo shirt that was so neat and tidy it might have come straight from the box. Nathan Powell's casualwear, she thought nastily.

"I didn't realize you were back." She glanced at his feet as she lied. Despite all her accomplishments, Jackie had never been able to manage an eyeball-to-eyeball lie.

"I haven't been for long." She was annoyed, Nathan realized. He found it enormously satisfying. Abandoning his rule against small talk, he smiled down at her. "So, how was your day?"

"Busy." Jackie pushed away from the side and began lazily treading water. In the east, the sky was nearly dark, but the last light from the sun touched the pool and garden. She didn't trust the way he was smiling right now, but she found she liked it. There was probably nothing more tedious than a man a woman could trust unconditionally. "And yours?"

"Relaxing." He had an urge, odd and unexpected, to slide into the pool with her. The water would be cool and soft; so would her skin. Maybe he was punchy, Nathan thought, after a hot day on the water.

As she continued to float, Jackie studied him. He did look relaxed—for him. She'd already discovered he was one of those people who carried around tension like a responsibility. She smiled, forgiving him as abruptly as she'd become angry.

"Want an omelet?"

"What?" Distracted, he pulled himself back. She was wearing two thin strips as an excuse for a bathing suit. The water, and perhaps a trick of the light, made them glimmer against her skin. A great deal of skin.

"Are you hungry? I could fix you an omelet."

"No. No, thanks." He took a sip of his drink to ease a suddenly dry throat, then sat the glass down to stuff his hands in his pockets. "It's cooling off." If that was the best he could do, he thought with a scowl, he'd best put the lid on small talk again.

"You're telling me." After sleeking her hair back, Jackie pulled herself out of the pool. She was skinny, Nathan told himself. There was no reason such a skinny, even lanky woman should move so athletically. In the fading sunlight, drops of water scattered over her skin like some primitive decoration.

"I forgot a towel." She shrugged, then shook herself. Nathan swallowed and looked elsewhere. It wasn't wise to look when he'd begun to imagine how easy it would be to slip those two tiny swatches of material off her and slide back into the water with her.

"I should go in," he managed after a moment. "I've got reading to catch up on."

"Me too. I'm reading tons of Westerns. Ever try Zane Grey or Louis L'Amour?" She was walking toward him as she spoke, and he found himself fascinated by the way the water clung to and darkened her hair and lashes. "Great stuff. I'll take this in for you."

"That's all right."

For the second time they reached at the same instant. For the second time their fingers touched and tangled. Nathan felt hers tense on the glass. So she felt it, too. That jolt... that connection, as he'd come to think of it. It wasn't his imagination. Wanting to avoid it, Nathan loosened his grip and stepped back. For the same reason, Jackie mirrored his move. The glass tipped, teetering on the edge of the table. They made the grab simultaneously, caught it, then stood holding the glass between them.

It should have been funny, she thought, but she managed only a quick, nervous laugh. In his eyes she saw exactly what she felt. Desire, hot and dangerous and edgy.

"Looks like we need a choreographer."

"I've got it." His voice was stiff as they waged a brief tug-of-war.

After relinquishing the glass to him, Jackie let out a slow, careful breath. She made the decision quickly, as she believed all the best decisions were made. "It might be better if we just got it over with."

"Got what over with?"

"The kiss. It's simple, really. I wonder what it would be like, you wonder what it would be like." Though her voice was casual, she moistened her lips. "Don't you think we'd be more comfortable if we stopped wondering?"

He set the glass down again as he studied her. It wasn't a romantic proposal, it was a logical one. That appealed to him. "That's a very pragmatic way of looking at it."

"I can be, occasionally." She shivered a little in the cooling air. "Look, odds are it won't be nearly as important after. Imagination magnifies things. At least mine does." The smile came again, quick and stunning, with the flash of a dimple at the corner of her mouth. "You're not my type. No offense. And I doubt I'm yours."

"No, you're not," he answered, stung a bit.

She took this statement with an agreeable nod. "So, we get the kiss out of the way and get back to normal. Deal?"

He didn't know if she'd done it on purpose—in fact, he was all but certain she hadn't—but she'd managed a direct hit to his male pride. She was so casual, so damn friendly about it. So sure that kissing him would leave her unaffected. Kissing him would be like brushing a pesky fly aside. Get it over with and get back to normal. He'd see about that.

She should have been warned by the look in his eyes—what she still thought of as his Jake look. Perhaps she had been, but it was knowledge gained too late.

With one hand he cupped her neck so that his fingers tangled in her dripping hair. The touch itself was a surprise—quietly intimate. There was a quick and sudden instinct to back away, but she ignored it. Jackie was used to approaching things head-on. So she stepped forward, tilting her head up. She expected something pleasant, warm, even ordinary. It wasn't the first time in her life she'd gotten more than she'd bargained for.

Rockets. They were her first image as his lips closed over hers. Rockets, with that flash of color and that fast, deadly boom. It had always been the boom she'd liked the best. Her little murmur wasn't of protest but of surprise and of pleasure. Accepting the pleasure, she leaned into him and absorbed it.

She could smell the water on him, not the clear, chlorinated water of the pool, but the darker, more exciting water that ran out to sea. The air was cooling rapidly as night fell, but the chill was gone. Her skin warmed as she moved against him and felt the soft brush of his shirt, and then of his hands.

And she *had* been waiting. The knowledge clicked quietly into place. She had been waiting years and years for this. Just this.

Unlike Jackie, Nathan had stopped thinking almost instantly—or thought he had. She tasted... exotic. There had been no warning of that in her pretty, piquant looks and wiry body, no indication of milk and honey heated with spice. She tasted of the desert, of something a dying man might drink greedily in the oasis of his mind.

He hadn't meant to hold her, not closely. He hadn't meant to let his hands roam over her, not freely. Somehow he'd lost control over them. With each touch and stroke over her damp skin, he lost a bit more.

Her back was long and lean and slick. He trailed his fingers over it and felt her tremble. The need jolted again until his mouth was hard on hers, more demanding than he'd ever intended. He pillaged. She accepted. When her sigh whispered against his tongue, his heartbeat doubled.

She pressed against him, her mouth open and willing, her body soft but not submissive. Her generosity was all-consuming. As was his temptation.

She'd never forget this, Jackie thought, not one detail. The heavy, heated scent of flowers, the soft hum of insects, the lapping of water close by. She'd never forget this first kiss, begun at dusk and carried into the night.

Her hands were in his hair, a smile just forming on her lips, as they drew apart. Unashamed of her reaction to him, she let out a long, contented sigh.

"I love surprises," she murmured.

He didn't. Nathan reminded himself of that and pulled back before he could stroke a hand through her hair. It amazed him and infuriated him to see that it wasn't steady. He wanted, unbearably, what he had no intention of taking.

"Now that we've satisfied our curiosity, we shouldn't have any more problems."

He expected anger. Indeed, that came first, a flash in her eyes. They were exceptionally expressive, he thought, and felt a pang when he read hurt in them. Then that, like the anger, disappeared, to be replaced by amusement.

"Don't bet the farm on it, Nathan." She patted his cheek—though she would have preferred to use her fist—and strolled into the house.

She was going to give him problems, all right, she thought as the screen door shut behind her. And it would be her pleasure.

Chapter Four

She would poison his poached eggs. Jackie could see the justice in that. He would come down for breakfast, cool-eyed and smug. She could even imagine what he'd be wearing—beige cotton slacks and a navy-blue shirt. Without a wrinkle in either.

She, giving him no reason to suspect, would serve him a lovely plate of Canadian bacon, lightly grilled, and poached eggs on toast. With a touch of cyanide.

He would sip his coffee. Nathan always went for the coffee first. Then he'd slice the meat. Jackie would fix herself a plate so everything would seem perfectly normal. They'd discuss the weather. A bit humid today, isn't it? Perhaps we're in for some rain.

As he took the first forkful of eggs, the sweat would break out cold on her brow as she waited...and waited.

In moments he would be writhing on the floor, gasping for air, clutching his throat. His eyes would be wide and shocked, then all too aware, as she stood over him, triumphant and smiling. With his last breath, he would beg for forgiveness.

But that wasn't subtle enough.

She was a great believer in revenge. People who forgave and forgot with a pious smile deserved to be stepped on. Not that she couldn't forgive small slights or unconscious hurts, but the big ones, the deliberate ones, required—no, demanded—payback.

She was going to give Nathan Powell the payback he deserved.

She told herself he was a cold fish, an unfeeling slug, a cardboard cutout. But she didn't believe it. Unfortunately for her, she'd seen the kindness and sense of fair play in him. Perhaps he was rigid, but he wasn't cold.

Maybe, just maybe, she had read too much into the kiss. Perhaps her emotions were closer to the surface than most people's, and there was a possibility that he hadn't heard the boom. But he'd felt something. A man didn't hold a woman as if he were falling off a cliff if he'd only slipped off a curb.

He'd felt something, all right, and she was going to see to it that he felt that and more. And suffered miserably.

She could take rejection, Jackie told herself as she ground fresh beans for coffee. Smashing something into dust gave her enormous satisfaction. Rejection was that part of life that toughened you enough to make you try harder. True, she hadn't had to deal with it very often, but she thought of herself as gracious enough to accept it when it was warranted.

Frowning, she watched the kettle begin to steam. It wasn't as though she expected men to fall at her feet—though she had enough ego to want one to trip a little now and again. She certainly didn't expect pledges of undying love and fidelity after one embrace, no matter how torrid.

But damn it, there had been something special between them, something rare and close to wonderful. He'd had no business turning it off with a shrug.

And he'd pay, she thought viciously as she poured boiling water over the ground coffee. He'd pay for the shrug, for the pretending disinterest, and more, he'd pay for the night she'd spent tossing in bed remembering every second she'd been in his arms.

It was a pity she wasn't stunning, Jackie mused as she heated a skillet. Really stunning, with razor-edged cheekbones and a statuesque build—or petite and fragile-looking, with melting blue eyes and porcelain skin. Frowning a bit, she tried to get a good look at her reflection in the stainless-steel range hood. What she saw was distorted and vague. Experimenting, she sucked in her cheeks, then let them out again with a puff of air.

Since her appearance was something she couldn't change, she would make the very best of what she had. Nathan Powell, man of stone and steel, would be eating out of her hand in no time.

She heard him come in but took her time before turning. The skimpy halter made the most of her tanned back. For the first time in days she'd raided her supply of makeup. Nothing jarring, she'd told herself. Just a bit of blush and gloss, with most of the accent on the eyes.

Jackie tossed one of her best smiles over her shoulders and had to stifle a shout of laughter. He looked dreadful. Wasn't that a shame?

He felt worse. While Jackie had been fuming and tossing in her bed, Nathan had been cursing and turning in his own. Her cheerful smile made him want to bare his teeth and snarl.

One kiss and they'd get back to normal? He'd have liked to strangle her. Things hadn't been normal since she'd forced herself into his life. As far as he could recall, his body hadn't ached like this since he'd been a teenager, when, fortunately, his imagination had outdistanced his experience. Now he knew exactly what it could be like and had spent most of the night thinking about it.

"Morning, Nate. Coffee?"

Nate? *Nate?* Because he was sure it would hurt too much to argue, he merely nodded.

"Hot and fresh, just the way you like it." If her voice had been any sweeter, she'd have grown wings. "We have Canadian bacon and eggs on the menu this morning. Ready in five minutes."

He downed the first cup. He set it back on the counter, and she filled it again. She'd used a freer hand with her scent. Her fragrance still wasn't rich or overpowering, but this morning it seemed just a bit more pungent than usual. Remember? it seemed to say. Cautious, he glanced up at her.

Did she look prettier, or was it just his imagination? How did she manage to make her skin always look so glowing, so soft? It wasn't right, it wasn't even fair, that her hair could be constantly disheveled and appealing whether she was tossing a salad or napping on his couch.

He'd have sworn he'd never seen anyone look so alive, so vivid, in the morning. It was infuriating that she should be so fresh when he felt as though he'd spent the night being pummeled by rubber-tipped sledgehammers.

Despite his best intentions, his gaze was drawn to her mouth. She'd put something on it, something that left it looking as moist and as warm as he remembered it tasted. Dirty pool, he thought, and scowled at her.

"Mrs. Grange is coming in today."

"Oh?" Jackie smiled at him again as she turned the sizzling bacon. "Isn't that nice? Things really are getting back to normal, aren't they?" Jackie broke an egg, one-handed, and dropped it in the poacher. "Do you plan to be here for lunch?"

The yolk didn't break, and the shell was neatly dispatched. A nice trick, Nathan thought. He was sure she had a million of them. "I'll be in all day. I've got a lot of calls to make."

"Good. I'll be sure to fix something special." She turned to him again to give him a long, interested study. "You know, Nathan, you look a little haggard this morning. Trouble sleeping?"

No matter how much it cost him, he wouldn't snarl. "I had some paperwork I wanted to clear up."

Jackie clucked her tongue sympathetically as she arranged his breakfast on a plate. "You work too hard. It makes you tense. You should try yoga. There's nothing like a little meditation and proper exercise to relax the body and mind.''

"Work relaxes me.''

"A common misconception.'' Jackie set the plate neatly in front of him, then scooted around the counter. "The fact is that work occupies your mind and can take your mind off other problems, but it doesn't cleanse. Take a good massage.''

Jackie began to knead his neck and shoulders while she spoke, pleased that at the first touch he jerked like a spring. "A really good massage,'' she continued as her fingers pressed and stroked, "relieves both mind and body of tension. A little oil, some soothing music, and you'll sleep like a baby. Oh, you've got yourself a real knot here at the base of your neck.''

"I'm fine,'' he managed. In another minute the fork he was holding was going to snap in two. She had magic in her hands. Black magic. "I'm never tense.''

Jackie frowned a moment, losing track of the purpose of the exercise. Did he believe that? she wondered. Probably. When a man was always tense, he obviously thought of it as normal. When her heart started to warm toward him, she lectured herself.

"Let's just say there's relaxed and there's relaxed.'' She concentrated on the teres minor. "After a really good rub, my muscles are like butter. I slide right off the table. I've got some wonderful oil. Hans swears by it.''

"Hans?'' Why was he asking? Nathan thought as, despite himself, he stretched under her hands.

"My masseur. He's from Norway and has the hands of an artist. He taught me his technique.''

"I'll just bet," Nathan muttered, and had Jackie grinning behind his back.

God, who would have suspected he had muscles like this? The man drew up blueprints and argued with engineers. Jackie hadn't suspected that his conservative shirts hid all those wonderful ridges. Last night, when he'd held her, she'd been too dazed to notice how well he was built. She ran her hands over his shoulders.

"You've got a terrific build," she told him. "I've got lousy deltoids myself. When I was into body-building, I never managed to do much more than sweat."

Enough was enough, Nathan thought. One more squeeze of those long, limber fingers and he'd do something embarrassing. Like whimpering. Instead, he spun around on the stool and caught her hands in his.

"What the hell are you trying to do?"

She didn't mind her heart skipping a beat. In fact, it was a delightful feeling. Still, she remembered that revenge was her first order of business.

"Just trying to loosen you up, Nate. Tension's bad for the digestion."

"I'm not tense. And don't call me Nate."

"Sorry. It suits you when you get that look in your eyes. That look," she explained, and she would have gestured if her hands hadn't been clamped in his. "The one that says shoot first and ask questions later."

He would be patient. Nathan told himself to count to ten, but only made it to four. "Careful, Jack.

You're here on probation. You'd be wise to back off from whatever game you're playing."

"Game?" She smiled, but her eyes held the first hint of frost he'd ever seen in them. For some reason, even that attracted him. "I don't know what you're talking about."

"What about that stuff you put on your mouth?"

"This?" Deliberately she ran her tongue over her upper, then her lower lip. "A woman's entitled to a little lipstick now and then. Don't you like it?"

He wouldn't dignify the question with an answer. "You put stuff on your eyes, too."

"Are cosmetics against the law in this state? Really, Nate—sorry, Nathan—you're being silly. Surely you don't think I'm trying to . . . seduce you?" She smiled again, daring him to comment. "I'd think a big strong man like you could take care of himself." She liked the way his eyes could darken from slate to smoke. "But if it stirs you up, I'll be certain to keep my mouth absolutely naked from now on. Will that be better?"

His voice was so soft, so very controlled, that she was fooled into thinking she was still at the wheel. "People who fight dirty end up in the mud themselves."

"So I've heard." She tossed back her head and looked at him from beneath her lashes. "But you see, I can take care of myself, too."

She saw then that she had misjudged him. Perhaps by no more than a few degrees, but such miscalculations could often be fatal. The look that came into his eyes was so utterly reckless, so coolly dangerous, that her heart thudded to a halt.

Jake was back, and his guns were smoking.

It would be more than a kiss now, whether she wanted it or not. It would be exactly as he chose, when he chose and how he chose. No amount of glib chatter or charming smiles was going to help.

When the doorbell rang, neither of them moved. With a hard, painful thump, Jackie's heart started again. Saved by the bell. She would have giggled if she hadn't been ready to collapse.

"That must be Mrs. Grange," she said brightly, just a shade too brightly. "If you'd let go of my hands now, Nathan, I'd be glad to answer the door while you finish your breakfast."

He did release her, but only after making her suffer through the longest five seconds of her life, during which she believed he would ignore the door and finish what his eyes had told her he intended to do. Saying nothing, Nathan let her go, then swiveled back around to the counter. The pity of it was that he no longer wanted coffee, but a nice stiff drink.

Jackie slipped out of the kitchen. She hoped his eggs were stone-cold.

She loved Mrs. Grange. When Jackie opened the door, she wasn't sure what to make of the large woman in the flowered housedress and high-top sneakers. Mrs. Grange gave Jackie a long, narrowed look with watery blue eyes, pursed her lips and said, "Well, well."

Understanding the implications of that, Jackie smiled and offered a hand. "Good morning. You must be Mrs. Grange. I'm Jack MacNamara, and Nathan's stuck with me for a few weeks because he can't bring himself to toss me out. Have you had breakfast?''

"An hour ago." After she stepped inside, Mrs. Grange set a huge canvas bag on the floor. "MacNamara. You must be related to that no-account."

Jackie didn't need a name. "Guilty. We're cousins. He's gone."

"And good riddance." With a sniff, Mrs. Grange cast a look around the living area. Though she approved of the fresh flowers, she was determined to withhold final judgment. "I'll tell you like I told him. I don't clean up after pigs."

"And who could blame you?" Jackie's grin was fast and brilliant. If dear cousin Fred had tried to charm Mrs. Grange, he'd fallen flat on his baby face. "I'm using the guest room, the blue-and-white one? I'm working in there, too, so if you'll just let me know where that room fits into your schedule I'll make sure I'm out of your way. I'm planning on fixing lunch about twelve-thirty," she continued, mentally adjusting her menu with the idea of carving a few pounds from Mrs. Grange's prodigious bulk.

Mrs. Grange's lips pursed again. It was a rare thing for an employer to offer her a meal. For the most part she was treated with polite, and bland, disregard. "I brought some sandwiches."

"Of course, if you'd rather, but I was hoping you'd join us. I'll be upstairs if you need anything. Nathan's in the kitchen and the coffee's fresh." She smiled again, then left Mrs. Grange to begin while she went upstairs.

Throughout the morning, Jackie heard the sounds of vacuuming and the heavy thud of Mrs. Grange's sneakers moving up and down the hallway. It pleased her that the noise and activity didn't intrude on her concentration. A real writer, in her opinion, should have imagination enough to overcome any outside interference. By noon, she was well on her way to sending Jake and Sarah on another adventure.

Jackie decided on a cracked-wheat-and-parsley salad for the lunch break. With the radio on, she set about dicing and cubing and humming to herself while she tried to imagine what it would be like to outrun desperadoes. When Nathan came in, she turned the music down, then set a huge bowl on the counter.

"Iced coffee all right?

"Fine." His answer was casual, but he was watching her. One wrong move, he thought, and he was going to pounce. He wasn't certain what would constitute a wrong move, or what he'd do once he'd pounced, but he was ready for her.

"I'd like to use the phone later, if you don't mind. Anything long-distance I'll charge to my credit card."

"All right."

"Thanks. I think it's about time to start planting the seeds of Fred's downfall."

With his fork halfway to his mouth, Nathan stopped. "What kind of seeds?"

"You're better off not knowing. Oh, hello, Mrs. Grange."

Annoyed with the interruption, Nathan turned to look at his housekeeper. "Mrs. Grange?"

"Sit down right here," Jackie said before Nathan could continue. "I hope you like this. It's called *tabouleh*. Very popular in Syria."

Mrs. Grange settled her bulk on a stool and eyed the bowl doubtfully. "It doesn't have any of that funny stuff in it, does it?"

"Absolutely not." Jackie set a glass of iced coffee next to the bowl. "If you like it, I'll give you the recipe for your family. Do you have a family, Mrs. Grange?"

"Boys are grown." Cautiously Mrs. Grange took the first forkful. Her hands, Jackie noticed, were work-reddened and ringless.

"You have sons?"

With a nod, Mrs. Grange dipped into the salad again. "Had four of them. Two of them are married now. Got three grandkids."

"Three grandchildren. That's marvelous, isn't it, Nathan? Do you have pictures?"

Mrs. Grange took another forkful. She'd never tasted anything quite like this. It wasn't cold meat loaf on rye, but it was nice. Real nice. "Got some in my bag."

"I'd love to see them." Jackie took a seat that set Mrs. Grange squarely between her and Nathan. He was eating in silence, like a man who found himself placed next to strangers at a diner. "Four sons. You must be very proud."

"They're good boys." Her wide, stern face relaxed a bit. "The youngest is in college. Going to be a teacher. He's smart, that one, never gave me a minute's trouble. The others..." She paused, then shook her head. "Well, that's what having kids is all about. This is a real nice salad, Miss MacNamara. Real pretty."

"Jack. And I'm glad you like it. Would you like some more coffee?"

"No, I'd best get back to work. You want me to take those shirts to the cleaners, Mr. Powell?"

"I'd appreciate it."

"If you don't need to use it now, I'll do your office."

"That's fine."

She turned to Jackie, and her eyes were friendly. "Don't worry about keeping out of the way upstairs. I can work around you."

"Thanks. Don't bother, I'll get these." She started to gather up bowls as Mrs. Grange plodded out. Nathan frowned at her over the rim of his iced coffee.

"What was all that about?"

"Hmm?" Jackie glanced at him as she transferred the leftover salad into a smaller dish.

"That business with Mrs. Grange. What were you doing?"

"Eating lunch. Would you mind if I gave her the rest of this to take home?"

"No, go ahead." He drew out a cigarette. "Do you usually have lunch with the help?"

She looked at him again, one brow lifting. "Why not?"

Every answer he thought of seemed stilted and snobbish, so he merely shrugged and lit his cigarette. Because she could see he was embarrassed, Jackie let it pass.

"Is Mrs. Grange divorced or widowed?"

"What?" Nathan blew out a stream of smoke and shook his head. "How would I know? How do you know she's either?"

"Because she talked about her sons and her grand-children, but she didn't mention her husband. Therefore it's elementary, my dear Nathan, that she hasn't got one." As an afterthought, she popped one last crouton into her mouth. "I opt for divorce because widows usually continue to wear a wedding ring. Hasn't it ever come up?"

"No." He brooded, staring into his coffee. For some reason he didn't want to confess that Mrs. Grange had worked for him for five—no, it was nearly six years now—and he hadn't known she had four sons and three grandchildren until five minutes ago. "It wasn't part of her job description, and I didn't want to pry."

"That's nonsense. Everyone likes to talk about their families. I wonder how long she's been single." She moved around the kitchen rinsing bowls, tidying counters. The rings on her fingers flashed with wealth, while her hands spoke of confidence. "I can't think of anything tougher than raising kids on your own. Do you ever think about that?"

"Think about what?"

"About having a family." She poured herself another glass with the idea of taking the coffee upstairs. "Thinking about kids always makes me feel very traditional. White picket fence, two-car garage, wood-paneled station wagon and all of that. I'm surprised you're not married, Nathan. Being a traditional man."

Her tone had him scowling. "I know when I've been insulted."

"Of course you do." She touched his cheek lightly with her fingertips. "Being traditional's nothing to be ashamed of. I admire you, Nathan, really I do. There's something endearing about a man who always knows where his socks are. When the right woman comes along, she's going to get a real prize.''

His hand clamped over her wrist before she could draw away. ''Have you ever had your nose broken?''

Absolutely delighted, she grinned at him. ''Not so far. Want to fight?''

''Let's try this.''

Jackie found herself sprawled over him as he sat on the stool. He'd caught her off balance, and she had to grab his shoulders to keep from falling on her face. She hadn't expected him to move that quickly, or precisely in that way. Before she could decide how to counter it—or whether she should counter it—his mouth was on hers. And it was searing.

He didn't know why he'd done it. What he'd really wanted to do, ached to do, was slug her. Of course, a man didn't slug a woman, so he'd really been left with no choice.

Why he'd thought a kiss would be revenge was beyond him now that it was begun. She didn't struggle, though he knew from the way her breath caught and her fingers tightened that he had at least surprised her.

But she couldn't have been more surprised than he.

Damn it, he wasn't the kind of man who yanked women around. Yet it seemed right when it was Jackie. It seemed ... fated. He could rationalize for hours, he could reason and deliberate until everything was crystal-clear. Then he could touch her and blow logic to smithereens.

He didn't want her. He was eaten up with wanting her. He didn't even like her. He was fascinated by her. He thought she was crazy. And he was beginning to be sure he was. Always he'd known there was a pattern to everything, a structure. Until Jackie.

He nipped his teeth into her bottom lip and heard her low, quiet moan. Apparently life wasn't always geometrical.

She'd asked for it, Jackie thought to herself. And, thank God, she'd gotten it. Thoughts of revenge, of making him suffer and sweat, flew out of her mind as she dived into the kiss. It was wonderful, sweet, sharp, hot, trembling, the way she'd imagined and hoped a kiss might be.

Her heart went into it, completely, trustingly. This was a man who could love her, accept her. She wasn't a fool, and she wasn't naive. She felt it from him as clearly as if he'd spoken the words. This was special, unique, the kind of loving poems were written about and wars were fought for. Some people waited a lifetime for only this. And not everyone found it. She knew it, and she wrapped her arms around him, ready to give him everything she was. No questions, no doubts.

Something was happening. Over the desire, over the passion, he could sense it. There was a change inside him, an opening, a recklessness. When her mouth was on his, her body melting in his arms, he couldn't think beyond the moment. That was crazy. He never thought of today without taking tomorrow into account. But now, just now, he could think only of holding her like this. Of tasting more of her, bit by slow bit. Of exploring her, discovering her. He couldn't think of anything but her.

It was insanity. He knew it, feared it, even as he pressed her closer. Sinking. He was sinking into her.

It was an odd and erotic sensation to feel himself lose his grip. He had to stop this, and stop it cold, before whatever was growing inside him grew too big to be controlled.

He drew her away, struggling to be firm, planning to be cruel. If she smiled at him instead of striking back, he knew, he'd be on his knees. He knew he should tell her all bets were off, to pack her things and leave. But he couldn't. No matter how much he told himself he wanted her out of his life, he couldn't ask her to go.

"Nathan." Aroused, pliant, already in love, she cupped her hand over his cheek. "Let's give Mrs. Grange the rest of the day off. I want to be with you."

Words caught in his throat, trapped in a fresh surge of desire. He'd never known a woman who was more open with her feelings, more honest with her needs. She scared him to death. He gave himself an extra moment. He couldn't afford to have his voice sound unsteady or to have her see how flexible his resolve was.

"You're getting ahead of yourself." As if the kiss had been only a kiss, he set her back on the floor. He hadn't realized how much warmth she'd brought to him until he'd no longer been touching her. "I don't think having an affair is in your best interests, or mine, considering our current arrangement. But thanks."

She went pale, and he knew that he'd gone too far in his rush for self-protection.

"Jackie, I didn't mean that the way it sounded."

"Didn't you? Well, whatever." She was amazed, absolutely amazed, at how much it hurt. She'd always dreamed of falling in love, deeply, blindly, beautifully in love. So this was how it felt, she thought as she pressed a hand to her stomach. The poets could keep it.

"Jack, listen—"

"No, I'd really rather not." When she smiled at him now, he realized just how special her genuine smile was. "No explanations required, Nathan. It was only a suggestion. I should apologize for coming on too strong."

"Damn it, I don't want an apology."

"No? Well, that's good, because I think I'd choke on it. I really should get back to work, but before I go there's just one thing." Deadly calm, Jackie picked up her glass of iced coffee and emptied it in his lap. "See you at dinner."

She worked like a maniac, barely noticing when Mrs. Grange came in to change the bed linen and dust the furniture. She was both amazed and infuriated at how close, how dangerously close, she'd been to tears. It wasn't that she minded shedding tears. There were times when she enjoyed nothing more than a wailing crying jag. But she knew that if she gave in to this one she wouldn't enjoy it a bit.

How could he have been so insensitive, so unfeeling, as to think she'd been offering him nothing more than sex, a quick afternoon romp? And how could she have been so stupid as to think she'd fallen in love?

Love took two people. She knew that. Wasn't she even now pouring her heart out in a story that involved two people's feelings and needs? And those feelings hadn't sprung out of a kiss but out of time and struggle.

Same old Jack, she accused herself. Still believing that everything in life came as easily as slipping off a log. She'd deserved a swift kick and had gotten one. But deserving or not, it didn't make it any less humiliating that Nathan had been the one to plant it.

Mrs. Grange cleared her throat for the third time as she fluffed Jackie's pillows. The minute the typewriter stilled, she stepped in.

"You sure do type fast," she began. "You do secretarial work?"

There was no reason to take out her foul mood on the housekeeper, Jackie reminded herself as she forced a smile. "No, actually I'm writing a book."

"Is that so?" Interested, Mrs. Grange walked to the foot of the bed to tug on the spread. "I like a good story myself."

Mrs. Grange was the first person Jackie had told about her writing who hadn't raised a brow or rolled her eyes. Encouraged, she swiveled around in her chair. The devil with Nathan, she thought. Jacqueline R. MacNamara had come to write a book, and that was just what she was going to do.

"Do you get much of a chance to read?"

"Nothing I like better after a day on my feet than to sit down with a nice story for an hour or two." Mrs. Grange edged a little closer, passing a dustrag over the lamp. "What kind of book are you writing?"

"A romance, a historical romance."

"No fooling? I'm partial to love stories. You been writing long?"

"Actually, this is my first try. I spent about a month doing research and compiling information and dates and things, then I just dived in."

Mrs. Grange shifted her gaze to the typewriter, then looked back at the lamp. "I guess it's like painting. You don't want anybody looking till it's all done."

"Are you kidding?" Laughing, Jackie tucked her feet under her. "I've been dying for somebody to want to read some of it." But not her family, Jackie thought, nibbling on her lower lip. They had already seen too much of what she'd begun, then left undone. "Want to see the first page?" Jackie was already whipping it from the pile and offering it.

"Well, now." Mrs. Grange took the typed sheet and held it out at arm's length until she focused on it. She read with her lips pursed and her eyes narrowed. After a moment she let out three wheezes that Jackie recognized as a laugh. Nothing, absolutely nothing, could have pleased her more.

"You sure did start out with a bang, didn't you?" There was both admiration and approval in Mrs. Grange's eyes as she looked over the end of the sheet. "Nothing like a gunfight to pique the interest."

"That's what I was hoping. Of course, it's just a first draft, but it's going fast." She accepted the page back and studied it. "I'm hoping to have enough to send off in a couple of weeks."

"I'l be mighty pleased to read the whole thing when you've finished."

"Me too." Jackie laughed again as she placed the first page on top of the pile. "Every day when I see how many pages I've done I can't believe it." A bit hesitantly, she laid her hand on top of the manuscript pages. "I haven't figured out what I'm going to do when it's all finished."

"Well, I guess you'll just have to write another one, won't you?" Bending, Mrs. Grange hefted her box of cleaning tools and clumped out.

Why, she was right, Jackie thought. Win or lose, life didn't begin or end on the first try. There couldn't be anyone who knew that better than herself. If something worked, you kept at it. And if something didn't work, and you wanted it, you kept right at that, too.

Turning around, she smiled at the half-typed page in her machine. She could apply that philosophy nicely to her writing. And while she was at it she might just apply it to Nathan.

Chapter Five

He was furious with himself. Still, it was easier, and a lot more comfortable, to turn his fury on her. He hadn't wanted to kiss her. She'd goaded him into it. He certainly hadn't wanted to hurt her. She'd forced him to do so. In a matter of days she'd turned him into a short-tempered villain with an overactive libido.

He was really a very nice man. Nathan was certain of it. Sure, he could be tough-minded, and he was often an impatient perfectionist on the job. He could hire and fire with impersonal speed. But that was business. In his personal life he'd never given anyone reason to dislike him.

When he saw a woman socially, he was always careful to see that the rules were posted up front. If the relationship deepened, both would be fully aware of its possibilities and its limitations. No one would ever have called him a womanizer.

Not that he didn't have a certain number of female . . . friends. It would be impossible for a grown man, a healthy man, to go through life without some companionship and affection. But, damn it, he made the moves, the overtures—and there was a certain flow to how these things worked. When a man and a woman decided to go beyond being friends, they did so responsibly, with as much caution as affection. By the time they did, if they did, they'd developed a certain rapport and understanding.

Groping in the kitchen after a parsley salad wasn't his idea of a sensible adult relationship.

If that was old-fashioned, then he was old-fashioned.

The problem was, that kiss over the kitchen counter had meant more, had shaken him more, than any of the carefully programmed, considerate and mature relationshps he'd ever experienced. And it wasn't the way he wanted his life to run.

He hadn't learned much from his father, other than how to knot a tie correctly, but he had learned that a woman was to be treated with respect, admiration and care. He was—always had been—a gentleman. Roses for the proper occasion, a light touch and a certain amount of courtship.

He knew how to treat a woman, how to steer a relationship along the right course and how to end one without scenes and recriminations. If he was overly careful not to allow anyone to get too close, he had good reason. Another thing he'd learned from his father, in reverse, was never to make promises he wouldn't keep or establish bonds he would certainly break. It had always been a matter of pride to him that whenever it had become necessary to end a relationship he and the woman involved had parted as friends.

How could he and Jackie part as friends when they hadn't yet become friends? In any case, Nathan considered himself sharp enough to know that if a relationship was begun, then ended, with a woman like Jackie, it wouldn't end without scenes or recriminations. The end, he was sure, would be just as explosive and illogical as the beginning.

He didn't like mercurial personalities or flash-fire tempers. They interfered with his concentration.

What he needed to do was to get back in gear—start the preliminaries on his next project, resume his social life. He'd spent too much time on the troubles and triumphs with the complex in Germany. Now that he'd gotten home, he hadn't had a peaceful moment.

His own fault. Nathan was willing to accept responsibility. His uninvited guest had another week—after all, she had his word on that. Then she was out. Out and forgotten. Well, out, in any case.

He started upstairs with the intention of changing and drowning himself in the pool. Then he heard her laugh. It was just his bad luck, he supposed, that she had such an appealing laugh. He heard her speak in that quicksilver way she had, and he stopped. Her bedroom door was open, and her voice raced out. It wasn't eavesdropping, he told himself. It was, after all, his house.

"Aunt Honoria, what in the world gave you that idea?" Kicked back in a chair, Jackie held the phone between her shoulder and chin as she painted her toenails. "Of course I'm not annoyed with Fred. Why should I be? He did me a wonderful favor." Jackie dipped her brush in the bottle of Sizzling Cerise polish and played her cards close to her chest. "The house is absolutely perfect, exactly what I'd been looking for, and Nathan—Nathan's the owner, darling—yes, he's just adorable."

She held her foot out to admire her handiwork. Between writing and cooking, she hadn't had time for a pedicure in weeks. No matter how busy, her mother would have said, a woman should always look her best from head to toe.

"No, dear, we've worked things out beautifully. He's a bit of a hermit, so we keep to ourselves. I'm fixing his meals for him. The darling's developing a bit of a paunch."

Outside the door, Nathan automatically reached a hand to his stomach.

"No, he couldn't be sweeter. We're rubbing along just fine. He might be one of my uncles. As a matter of fact, his hairline's receding just like Uncle Bob's."

This time both of Nathan's hands went to his hair.

"I'm just glad I could put your mind at ease. No, be sure to let Fred know everything couldn't be better. I'd have gotten in touch with him myself, but I wasn't sure just where he'd popped off to."

There was a pause. For some reason, Nathan felt it was a particularly cold one.

"Of course, dear, I know exactly how our Fred is."

In the hallway, Nathan heard little murmurs of agreement and a few light laughs. He was just about to continue when Jackie spoke again.

"Oh, Aunt Honoria, I nearly forgot. What was the name of that wonderful realtor you used on the Hawkins property?"

Jackie switched feet and moved in for the kill.

"Well, dear, it's rather confidential still, but I know I can trust you. It seems there's this block of land, about twenty-five acres. South of here, a place called Shutter's Creek. Yes, it is rather precious, isn't it? In any case…you will keep this to yourself, won't you?"

Jackie smiled and continued to paint as she received her aunt's assurances. Aunt Honoria's promises were as easily smeared as wet nail polish. "Yes, I knew you would. Anyway, it's being sold at rock bottom, and naturally I wouldn't have been interested. Who would? It's hardly more than a swamp at this point. But the beauty is, dear, that Allegheny Enterprises—you know, the contractors who put up all those marvelous resorts? Yes, that's the one. They're scouting out the location. They're thinking about pumping it and filling it in and putting up one of those chichi places like they did in Arizona. Yes, it was marvelous what they did with a few acres of desert, wasn't it?"

She listened a few more moments, knowing how to play a line until the bait was well taken.

"Just a little tip from a friend of mine. I want to snap it up quickly then resell it to Allegheny. Word from my friend is that they'll pay triple the asking price. Yes, I know, sounds too good to be true. Do keep this under your hat, auntie. I want to see if I can have the realtor rush this through settlement before the lid's off."

Jackie listened for a moment as she debated putting on a third coat.

"Yes, it could be exciting, and very hush-hush. That's why I don't want to tip my hand to the realtor here in Florida. No, I haven't said a thing to Mother and Daddy yet. You know how I love surprises. Oh, darling, there's the door. Must run. Do give my best to everyone. I'll be in touch. *Ciao*."

Delighted with herself, Jackie stretched in the chair and sent it spinning in a circle.

"Well, hello, Nathan."

"I don't know where you get your information," he began, "but unless you want to lose even more money, I'd look for someplace other than Shutter's Creek. It's twenty-five acres of sludge and mosquitoes."

"Yes, I know." With the ease of the limber, Jackie brought her leg around so that she could blow on her painted toenails. Nathan wouldn't have been surprised if she'd tucked her heel behind her ear and grinned at him. "And unless I miss my guess, dear old Fred will own all those lovely mosquitoes within forty-eight hours." Smiling at Nathan, she pillowed her head on her folded arms. "I always figure when you pay back you should pay back where it'll hurt the most. For Fred, that's his wallet."

Impressed, Nathan stepped farther into the room. "You planted the seeds of his downfall?"

"Exactly, and like Jack's beanstalk, it should sprout overnight."

Nathan mulled it over. It was a nasty trick, a very nasty trick. He only wished he'd thought of it. "How do you know he'll go for it?"

Jackie merely continued to smile. "Want to make a wager on it?"

"No," he said after a moment. "No, I don't think I do. How much are they asking an acre?"

"Oh, only two thousand. Fred should be able to beg, borrow or steal fifty without too much trouble." Deciding against a third coat, she capped the bottle. "I always pay my debts, Nathan. Without exception."

He was aware he'd been warned and decided he deserved it. "If it's any consolation, I doubt I'll be able to drink iced coffee again."

She crossed her legs lazily. "I suppose that's something."

"And I'm not losing my hair."

She flicked her gaze over it. It was thick and full and dark. She could remember with absolute clarity how it had felt between her fingers. "Probably not."

"Nor do I have a paunch."

With her tongue caught between her teeth, she let her glance slide down to his taut and very flat stomach. "Well, not yet."

"And I am not adorable."

"Well..." Her eyes were laughing when they came back to his. "Cute, then—in a staid and very masculine sort of way."

He opened his mouth to argue, then decided it was safer to give up. "I'm sorry," he said instead before he knew he'd meant to tell her.

Jackie's eyes softened along with her smile. Revenge always took a back seat to an apology. "Yes, I think you are. Do you like fresh starts, Nathan?"

So it was that easy. He should have known it would be that easy with her. "Yes, actually, I do."

"All right, then." She unwound herself from the chair. If he found himself looking at her legs again, he was only human. When she stood, she offered a hand. "Friends?"

He knew he could have given her a list of reasons they couldn't be, certainly a lengthy one of reasons why they shouldn't be. But he put his hand in hers. "Friends. Do you want to take a swim?"

"Yeah." She could have kissed him. God, she wanted to. Lecturing herself, Jackie smiled instead. "Give me five minutes to change."

She took less than that. When she arrived, Nathan was just surfacing. Before he had the chance to shake the water out of his eyes and spot her, she dived in beside him. She came up cleanly, head tilted back so that her hair was slick against her head.

"Hi."

"You move fast."

"Mostly." She moved into a smooth sidestroke and did a length and a half. "I love your pool. That helped sell me on the place, you know. I grew up with a pool, so I'd have hated to spend three months without one."

"Glad I could oblige," he told her, but it didn't come out nearly as sarcastic as he'd expected. She smiled and switched to a breaststroke that barely rippled the water. "I take it you do a lot of swimming."

"Not as much as I used to." With what looked like no effort at all, she rolled onto her back to float. "I was on a swim team for a couple of years in my teens. Gave some serious thought to the Olympics."

"I'm not surprised."

"Then I fell in love with my swim coach. His name was Hank." She sighed and closed her eyes on the memory. "I couldn't seem to concentrate on my form after that. I was fifteen and Hank was twenty-five. I imagined us married and raising a relay team. He was only interested in my backstroke. I've always been able to go backward well."

"You don't say."

"No, really. I was all-state with my backstroke. Anyway, Hank was about five-eight, with shoulders like I beams. I've always been a sucker for shoulders." She opened her eyes briefly to study him. Without a shirt, his body seemed tougher and more disciplined than she had expected. "Yours are very nice."

"Thanks." He discovered it was both relaxing and invigorating to float beside her.

"Also, Hank had the greatest blue eyes. Like lanterns. I wove some wonderful fantasies around those eyes."

Irrationally he began to detest Hank. "But he was only interested in your backstroke."

"Exactly. To get him to notice me, I pretended I was drowning. I imagined him pulling me out and doing mouth-to-mouth until he realized he was madly in love and couldn't live without me. How was I supposed to know that my father had picked that day to come in and watch practice?"

"No one could have."

"I knew you'd understand. So there's my father jumping into the pool in his three-piece wool suit and Swiss watch. Neither were ever quite the same again, by the way. By the time he dragged me to the side he was hysterical. Some of my teammates thought it was a reaction from shock, but my father knew me too well. Before I could blink, I was off the swim team and on the tennis courts. With a female pro.''

"Your father sounds like a very wise man.''

"Oh he's as sharp as they come, J. D. Mac-Namara. No one's ever been able to put anything over on him for long. God knows I've tried.'' She sighed and let the water lap around her. ''He'll get a tremendous charge out of it when I tell him about the sting I pulled on Fred.''

"You're close to your family?''

Jackie thought, but couldn't be sure, that his voice sounded wistful. "Very. Sometimes almost too much, which may be why I'm always pulling myself off somewhere to try something new. If Daddy had his way, I'd be safely housed in Newport with the man of his choice, raising his grandchildren and keeping out of trouble. Do you have any family here in Florida?''

"No.''

She didn't have any doubts about it this time. The subject was definitely on posted ground. Not wanting to irritate him again so soon, Jackie let it pass. "Want to race?''

"Where?'' He nearly yawned as he said it. He couldn't remember the last time he'd been so completely relaxed.

"To one end and back to the other. I'll give you a three-stroke lead.''

He opened his eyes at that. Jackie was treading water now, her face only inches from his. As he looked at her, Nathan realized he could yank her to him and have his mouth on hers in a heartbeat. Racing, he decided, was a much better idea.

"Fine." He took three easy strokes, then saw the bullet pass him. Amused, and challenged, he kicked in.

It might have been a few years since she'd been on a swim team, but after five yards Nathan saw that she'd retained her competitive spirit. With some women, with most women, he'd have been inclined to lose, knowing that the woman involved would know he'd done so purposely.

He didn't feel inclined to lose to Jackie.

When they touched the wall and rolled into a turn, they were head-to-head. He couldn't, as he'd expected, sprint ahead of her. Her long legs propelled her forward, and her slim arms cut through the water in quick, smooth strokes. Gradually he inched ahead, one stroke, then two, with the advantage of his longer reach. When they came to the side he touched only half a body length ahead.

"I must be slipping." A little breathless, Jackie leaned her forearms on the edge, pillowed her cheek on them and studied him. His skin was shiny with water now, drops running off of and clinging to muscular forearms and shoulders. The kind of arms and shoulders, Jackie thought, that a woman could depend on. "You're in good shape, Nathan."

"You too." He was out of breath himself.

"No handicap next time."

He grinned. "I'll still beat you."

"Maybe." Jackie dragged a hand through her hair so that it curled, wet and charming, around her face. "How's your tennis?"

"Not bad."

"Well, that's a possibility." She pulled herself up and out, then sat on the edge, legs dangling. "How about Latin?"

"What about Latin?"

"We could have a Latin tournament."

With a shake of his head, he pulled himself up to sit beside her. "I don't know any Latin."

"Everyone knows some Latin. Corpus delicti or magna cum laude." She leaned back on her elbows. "I can never understand why they call it a dead language when it's used every day."

"That's certainly something to think about."

She laughed. She couldn't help it. He had such a droll way of telling her he thought she was crazy. When his eyes were light and friendly and the smile was beginning to play around his mouth, he seemed like someone she'd known all her life. Or wished she had.

"I like you, Nathan. I really do."

"I like you, too. I think." It wasn't possible not to smile back at her, just as it wasn't possible not to look at her if she was anywhere nearby. She drew you in. Being with her was like plunging into a cold lake on a sultry day. It was a shock to the system, but a welcome one.

Before he realized what he was doing, Nathan reached over to tuck a dripping curl behind her ear. It wasn't like him; he didn't touch casually. The moment his fingers brushed her cheek he knew it was just one more mistake. How could you want more when you weren't even certain what it was you were taking?

As he started to draw away, she leaned up just a little and took his hand in hers. She brought his fingers to her lips in a gesture that stunned him with the naturalness of it.

"Nathan, is there some woman I should be concerned about?"

He didn't pull away, though he knew he should. Somehow his fingers had curled with hers and were holding on. "What do you mean?"

"I mean, you said you weren't involved, but I wondered if there was someone. I don't mind competing, I just like to know."

There was no one. Even if there had been, her memory would have vanished like a puff of smoke. That was what worried him. "Jack, you're taking two steps to my one."

"Am I?" She shifted. It only took a small movement to have her lips whisper against his. She didn't press, content for now with only a taste. "How long do you think it'll take you to catch up?"

He didn't remember moving, but somehow his hands were framing her face. He could feel the water turning to steam on his skin. It should have been easy, uncomplicated. She was willing, he was desirous. They were adults who understood the rules and the risks. There were no promises between them, and no demands for any.

But even as her lips parted beneath his, even as he took what she offered and ached for more, he knew there would be nothing simple about it.

"I don't think I'm ready for you," he murmured, but lowered her onto the concrete apron of the pool.

"Then don't think." Her arms went around him. She'd been waiting. There was no way she could explain to him that she'd been waiting for him, just for him, all her life. It was so easy, so natural, to want him and to give in to that wanting.

Somehow, even as a girl, she'd known there would only be one man for her. She hadn't known how or when she'd find him, or even if she would. Without him, she would have been content to live on her own, satisfying herself with the love of family and friends. Jackie had never believed in settling for second best.

But now he was here, his mouth on her mouth, his body warming hers. She didn't have to think about tomorrow or the day after that when she was holding a lifelong dream in her arms.

What she wanted was here and now. Turning into him, Jackie murmured his name and cherished the sensation of being wanted in turn.

She wasn't like other women. But why? He'd wanted before, been charmed and baffled and achy before. But not like this. He couldn't think when he was close to her. He could only feel. Tenderness, passion, frustration, desire. It was as if when he held her intellect clicked off and emotion, pure emotion, took over.

Was it that she was every man's fantasy? A generous, willing woman with needs and demands to match a man's—a woman without inhibitions or pretenses. He wished he could believe it was that. He wanted to believe it was only that. But he knew it was more. Somehow it was much more.

And he was losing himself, degree by degree, layer by layer. All his life he'd known where he was going and why. It wasn't possible, it wasn't right, to allow this—to allow her—to change it.

He had to stop it now, while he still had a choice, or at least while he could still pretend he had one.

Slowly, and with much more difficulty than he'd imagined, he pulled away from her. The sun was hanging in the west, still bright, vivid enough to bring out the highlights in her hair. It wasn't just brown as he'd thought, it had dozens and dozens of variations of the shade. Soft, warm, rich. Like her eyes. Like her skin.

He forced himself not to lift a hand to her cheek to touch just once more.

"We'd better go in."

She'd melted inside. Completely. He could have asked anything of her in that moment and she'd have given it without a second thought. Such was the power of loving. She blinked, struggling against coming back to earth. If the choice had been hers, and hers alone, she would have stayed where she was, in his arms, forever.

But she wasn't a fool. He wasn't talking about going in to continue what they'd begun, but to end it. She closed her eyes, accepting the hurt.

"Go ahead. I think I'll get a little more sun."

"Jack."

She opened her eyes. He was surprised to see such patience in them. He shifted away, knowing that if he remained too close he'd touch her again and start the merry-go-round spinning. "I don't like to start anything until I know how it's going to finish."

She let out a long sigh because she understood. "That's too bad. You miss an awful lot that way, Nathan."

"And make less mistakes. I don't like to make mistakes."

"Is that what I am?" There was just enough amusement in her voice for him to be relieved.

"Yes. You've been a mistake right from the beginning." He turned to her again, noting that she was looking at him the way he sometimes saw her look when she was putting together a complicated dish. "You know it would be better if you didn't stay here."

She lifted a brow. It was the only change in the quietly intense look. "Are you kicking me out?"

"No." He said it too quickly and cursed himself for it. "I should, but I don't seem to be able to."

She laid a hand on his shoulder lightly. He was tense again. "You want me, Nathan. Is that so terrible?"

"I don't take everything I want."

She frowned a moment, thinking. "No, you wouldn't. You're too sensible. It's one of the things I like best about you. But you will take me eventually, Nathan. Because there's something right about us. And we both know it."

"I don't sleep with every woman who attracts me."

"I'm glad to hear it." Jackie sat up completely, tucked up her knees and wrapped her arms around them. "Indulging like that is dangerous in more ways than one." Turning her head, she studied him. "Do you think I sleep with every man who raises my blood pressure?"

Restless and not entirely comfortable, he moved his shoulders. "I don't know you or your life-style."

"Well, that's fair." She preferred things to be fair. "Let's get the sex out of the way, then. It dims the romance a bit, but it's sensible. I'm twenty-five, and I've fallen in and out of love countless times. I like falling in better, but I've never been able to stick. Nathan, this might be difficult for you to accept, but I'm not a virgin."

When he shook his head and dropped his chin on his chest, she patted his shoulder.

"I know, shocking, isn't it? I confess, I've been with a man. Actually, I've been with two. The first time was on my twenty-first birthday."

"Jack—"

"I know," she interrupted with a wave of her hand. "That's a little late in this day and age, but I hate to follow trends. I was crazy about him. He could quote Yeats."

"That explains it," Nathan muttered.

"I knew you'd understand. Then a couple of years ago I was into photography. Moody black-and-whites. Very esoteric. I met this man. Black leather jacket. Very sullen good looks." There was more amusement in her eyes now than sentiment.

"He moved in with me and sat around being attractive and despondent. It only took me a couple of weeks to discover I wasn't meant to be depressed. But I got some wonderful pictures. Since then, there hasn't been anyone who's made my toes curl. Until you."

He sat still, wondering why he should be glad there had only been two important men in her life. And why he was now jealous of both of them. After a moment he looked at her again. The light had changed subtly. It warmed her skin now.

"I can't decide whether you have no guile whatso-ever or if you have more than anyone I've ever met."

"Isn't it nice to have something to wonder about? I guess that's why I want to write. You can 'I wonder' yourself from beginning to end." She was silent only a moment. Jackie's debates with herself never lasted long. "Nathan, there's another thing you might want to wonder about. I'm in love with you."

She rose after she told him, feeling it would be best for both of them.

"I don't want you worry about it," she said as he sat in stunned silence. "It's just that I hate it when people try to pretend things away. Good things, I mean. I think I'll go in after all and change before I start dinner."

She left him alone. He wondered if anyone else could drop a bombshell so casually, then wander off without checking the damage. Jackie could.

He frowned, watching the way the sun danced in diamonds on the water. There was a boat running north. He could just hear the purr of the motor. The air smelled richly of spring, flowers sun-warmed and burgeoning, grass freshly cut. The days were lengthening, and the heat remained well into evening.

That was life. It went on. It had a pattern.

She was in love with him.

That was absurd . . . so why wasn't he surprised? It all had to do with who she was, he decided. While he wasn't one to use words like love casually, she would be much freer with words, and with feelings.

He didn't even know what love meant to her. An attraction, an affection, a spark. That would be more than enough for many people. She was impetuous.

Hadn't she just told him she'd fallen in and out of love countless times? This was just one more adventure for her.

Wasn't that what he wanted to believe? If it was, why did the thought leave him cold and angry?

Because he didn't want to be another adventure. Not for her. He didn't want her to be in love with him... but if she was, he wanted it to be real.

Rising, Nathan walked over to where his land gave way to the wall and the wall to the water. Once his life had moved that smoothly—like a calm channel flowing effortlessly out to sea. That was what he wanted, and that was what he had. He didn't have time to deal with impulsive women who talked about love and romance.

Sometime in the future there would be time for such things—with the proper woman. Someone sensible and polished, Nathan thought. Then he wondered why that suddenly sounded like a nice piece of furniture instead of a wife.

She was doing this to him, he realized, and he resented it. She had no business telling him she was in love with him, making him think that maybe, just maybe, what he was feeling was—

No. He brought himself up short as he turned to scowl back at his house. It was beyond ridiculous to imagine, even for an instant, that he could be in love with her. He barely knew the woman, and for the most part she was an annoyance. If he was attracted it was simply because she was attractive. And he'd kept himself so tied up with work in Germany that he hadn't had time for the softer things a man needed.

And, damn it, that was a lie. Disgusted, he turned back to the water again. He did feel something for her. He wasn't sure what or why, but he felt it. He wanted more than to tumble into bed with her and satisfy an itch. He wanted to be with her, hold her, let that low, fascinating voice drain away his tensions.

But that wasn't love, he assured himself. It might have been a little like caring. That was almost acceptable. A man could come to care for a woman without sinking in over his head.

But not a woman like Jackie.

Dragging a hand through his hair, he started back to the house. They weren't going to talk about this, not now, and not later. Whatever it took, he was going to get back to normal.

He told himself it was expedient, not cowardly, to go in through the side door and avoid her.

Chapter Six

Jackie wasn't ashamed of having told Nathan what she felt. Nor did she wish the words back. One of her firmest beliefs was that it was useless to second-guess a decision once it had been made.

In any case, taking the words back or regretting them wouldn't change the fact that they were true. She hadn't meant to fall in love with him, which made it all the sweeter and more important. At other times in her life she had seen a man, thought that he might be the one and set about falling in love.

With Nathan, love had come unexpectedly, without plan or consideration. It had simply happened, as she had always secretly hoped it would. In her heart she'd known that love couldn't be planned, so she'd begun to believe that it would never be there for her.

He was not the perfect match for her, at least not in the way she'd once imagined. Even now she couldn't be sure he had all the qualities she had sometimes listed as desirable in a man.

None of that mattered, because she loved him.

She was willing to give him time—a few days, even a week—to respond in whatever way suited him. As far as she was concerned, there were no doubts as to how things would resolve themselves. She loved him. Fate had taken a hand, in the person of cousin Fred, and tossed them together. Perhaps Nathan didn't know it yet. As she whipped eggs for a soufflé, Jackie smiled. In fact, she was sure Nathan didn't know it yet, but she was exactly what he needed.

When a man was logical, conservative and—well, yes, even just a tad stuffy—he needed the love and understanding of a woman who wasn't any of those things. And that same woman—herself, in this case— would love the man, Nathan, because he was all the things he was. She would find his traits endearing and at the same time not allow him to become so starched he cracked down the middle.

She could see exactly the way it would be for them over the years. They would grow closer with an understanding so keen that each would be able to know what the other was thinking. Agreement wouldn't always be possible, but understanding would. He would work at his drawing board and attend his meetings, while she wrote and took occasional trips to New York to lunch with her publisher.

When his work took him away, she'd go with him, supporting his career just as he would support hers. While he supervised the construction of one of his buildings, she would fill reams of notebooks with research.

Until the children came. Then, for a few years, they would both stay closer to home while they raised their family. Jackie didn't want to imagine boys or girls or hair color, because something that precious should be a surprise. But she was sure that Nathan would be a marshmallow when it came to his children.

And she would be there for him, always, to knead the tension from his shoulders, to laugh him out of his sullen moods, to watch his genius grow and expand. With her, he would smile more. With him, she would become more stable. She would be proud of him, and he of her. When she won the Pulitzer they would drink a magnum of champagne and make love through the night.

It was really very simple. Now all she had to do was wait for him to realize how simple.

Then the phone rang.

With her mixing bowl held in the crook of her elbow, Jackie picked up the receiver from the wall unit. "Hello."

After a brief hesitation came a beautifully modulated voice. "Yes, is this the Powell residence?"

"Yes, it is. May I help you?"

"I'd like to speak to Nathan, please. This is Justine Chesterfield calling."

The name rang a bell. In fact, it rang several. Justine Chesterfield, the recently divorced darling of the society pages. The name opened doors in Bridgeport, Monte Carlo and St. Moritz. All in the proper season, naturally. Jackie believed in premonitions, and she didn't care for the one she was having at the moment.

She was tempted to hang up, but she didn't think that would solve anything.

"Of course." Her mother would have been delighted with the richly rounded tones. "I'll see if he's available, Mrs. Chesterfield."

It was ridiculous to be jealous of a voice over the phone. Besides, she didn't have a jealous bone in her body. Regardless, Jackie gained enormous satisfaction from sticking her tongue out at the receiver before she went to find Nathan.

Since he was just coming down the stairs, she didn't have to look far. "You have a phone call. Justine Chesterfield."

"Oh." He had a flash of guilt that baffled him. Why should receiving a call from an old friend make him feel guilty? "Thanks. I'll take it in my office."

She didn't linger in the hall. Not on purpose, anyway. Could she help it if she had a sudden and unavoidable itch on the back of her knee? So she stood, scratching, while Nathan stepped into his office and picked up the phone.

"Justine, hello. A few days ago. A new housekeeper? No, that was . . ." How did he, or anyone, explain Jackie? "Actually, I've been meaning to call you. Yes, about Fred MacNamara."

When she decided that if she scratched much longer she'd draw blood, Jackie wandered back into the kitchen. Once there, she stared at the phone. It would be easy to pick up the receiver, very slowly, very quietly—just to see if he was still on the line, of course.

She began to, and very nearly did. Then, with a muttered oath, she set it back on the hook. Audibly.

She wasn't interested in anything he had to say to *that woman*. Already Justine had taken on an italicized quality in her mind. Let him explain to *her* why he had a woman living with him. Because the idea amused her, Jackie turned up the radio a little louder and began to sing along with it.

With the care of a woman who loved to cook, she continued to mix the soufflé. She wouldn't slam pots and pans around the kitchen. Jackie knew how to control herself. She didn't make a habit of it, but she knew how. It was only a phone call, after all. As far as Jackie knew, *that woman* had phoned Nathan to make a plug for her favorite charity. Or maybe she wanted to remodel her den. There were a dozen very innocent and perfectly logical reasons for Justine Chesterfield to call Nathan.

Because she wants to get her hooks into him, Jackie thought, and made herself pour the soufflé mixture into the pan without spilling a drop.

"Jackie?"

She turned, as careful with her smile as she'd been with the batter. "All done? Did you have a nice chat with Justine?"

"I wanted to let you know I'll be going out so you wouldn't worry about dinner."

"Mm-hmm." Without missing a beat, Jackie set a cucumber on the chopping block and began to slice it. "I wonder, did Justine's second—or is it third—divorce ever come through?"

"As far as I know." He paused a moment, leaning against the doorjamb as he watched Jackie bring the knife down with deadly accuracy. Jealousy, he thought, recognizing it when it slammed into his face. He had a jealous woman on his hands, through no fault of his own. Nathan opened his mouth, then shut it again. He'd be damned if he'd explain himself. Perhaps it was absurd, but if she thought he and Justine were romantically involved it might be the best thing for everyone. "I'll see you later."

"Have a good time," she said, and brought the knife down with a satisfying *thwack*.

Jackie didn't turn, nor did she stop her steady slicing until she heard the front door shut. Blowing the hair out of her eyes, she poured the soufflé mixture down the drain. She'd eat a hot dog.

It helped to get back to work, to hear the comforting hum of her typewriter. What helped even more was the development of a new character. Justine—make that Carlotta—was the frowsy, scheming, over-endowed madam of the local brothel. Her heart was brass, like her hair. She was a woman who used men like poker chips.

Jake, being only a man, was taken in by her. But Sarah, with the clear eyes of a woman, saw Justine—Carlotta—for exactly what she was.

Afraid of his growing feelings for Sarah, Jake turned to Carlotta. The cad. Eventually Carlotta would betray him, and her betrayal would nearly cost Sarah her life, but for now Sarah had to deal with the fact that the man she'd come to love would turn to another woman to release his passion.

Jackie would have preferred to make Carlotta frumpy and faded. She'd even toyed with a wart. Just a small one. But a hard-faced woman wouldn't do justice to Jake or her book. Dutifully tearing up the first page, Jackie got down to business.

Carlotta was stunning. In a cold, calculated sort of way. Jackie had seen Justine's picture often enough to describe her. Pale and willowy, with eyes the clear blue of a mountain lake and a thin, almost childish mouth. A slender neck and wheat-blond hair. There were ice-edged cheekbones and balletic limbs. Taking literary license, Jackie allowed herself to toughen the looks, add a few dissipated lines and a drinking problem.

As she wrote, she began to see the character more clearly, even began to understand Carlotta's drive to use and discard men, to make a living off their baser drives and weaknesses. She discovered that Carlotta had had a miserable childhood and an abusive first marriage. Unfortunately, this softened her mood toward Justine even as she had Carlotta plotting dreadful problems for Jake and Sarah.

When Jackie ran out of steam, it was still shy of midnight. Telling herself it had nothing to do with waiting up for Nathan, she dawdled, applying a facial she remembered once or twice a month at best, filing her nails and leafing through magazines.

At one she deliberately turned the bedside light off, then lay staring at the ceiling.

Maybe everyone was right after all. Maybe she *was* crazy. A woman who fell in love with a man who had virtually no interest in her had to be asking for trouble. And heartache. This was her first experience with real heartache, and she couldn't say she cared for it.

But she did love him, with all the energy and devotion she was capable of. It wasn't anything like the way

it had been with the Yeats buff or the leather jacket.
They had brought on a sense of excitement—the way
a runner might feel, she thought, when she was about
to race the fifty-yard dash full-out. It was different,
very different, from preparing for a marathon. The
excitement was still there, but with it was a steady determination that came from the knowledge of being
ready to start and finish, of being prepared for the
long haul.

Like her writing, Jackie thought, and sat up in bed.
The parallel was so clear. With all her other projects
there had been that quick, almost frantic flash of energy and power. It had been as if she'd known going
in that there would be a short, perhaps memorable
thrill, then disenchantment.

With the writing, there had been the certainty that
this was it for her. It hadn't been her last chance so
much as her only one. What she was beginning now
was the one thing she'd been looking for through all
the years of experimenting.

Falling for Nathan was precisely the same. Other
men she'd cared for had been like stepping-stones or
springboards that had boosted her up for that one and
only man she would want for the rest of her life.

If someone had gotten in the way of her and her
writing, would she have tolerated it? Not for a minute. Mentally pushing up her sleeves, she settled back.
No one was going to step in the way of her and her
man, either. Justine Chesterfield was going to have a
fight on her hands.

He'd been home for nearly an hour, but Nathan sat
in his parked car and let the smoke from his cigarette

trail out the window. It was an odd thing for a man to be wary about going into his own house, but there it was. She was in there. In the bedroom. Her bedroom now. It would never be just a guest room again.

He'd seen her light burning, and he'd seen her light shut off. She might be sleeping. He wasn't sure he'd ever get a decent night's sleep again.

My God, he wanted to go in, walk up the stairs into her room and lose himself in the promise of her. Or the threat.

There was nothing in his feelings for her that made sense, nothing he could put his finger on and analyze. Over and over again his mind played back the way she'd looked at him as they'd sat by the pool, the way her skin had felt with water drying on it, the way her voice had sounded.

I'm in love with you.

Could it be, could it possibly be that easy for her? Yes, he thought it was. Now that he was beginning to know and understand her, he was sure that falling in love and declaring that love would be as natural for Jackie as breathing. But this time she was in love with him.

He could take advantage of it. She wouldn't even blame him for it. He could, without conscience or guilt, do exactly what he was dreaming of doing— walk into her room and finish what had been started that evening.

But he couldn't. He'd never be able to forget the way her eyes had looked. Trusting, honest and incredibly vulnerable. She thought she was tough, resilient. And he believed that she was, to a point. If she really loved him and he hurt her by casually taking what love urged her to give, she wouldn't bounce back.

So how did he handle her?

He'd thought he'd known earlier that evening. Going to see Justine had been a calculated move to distance himself from Jackie and to show both her and himself how ridiculously implausible any relationship between them would be.

Then he'd found himself in Justine's elegant condo with its gold-and-white rooms and its tasteful French antiques and he'd been unable to think of anything but Jackie. There'd been an excellent poached salmon, prepared to a turn by Justine's housekeeper. Nathan had found himself with a yen for the spicy chicken Jackie had prepared that first night.

He'd smiled as Justine, dressed in sleek white lounging pajamas, her wheat-colored hair twisted back in a sleek knot, had served him brandy. And he'd thought of the way Jackie looked in shorts.

With Justine he'd discussed mutual friends and compared viewpoints on Frankfurt and Paris. Her voice was low and soothing, her observations concise and mildly amusing. He'd rememberd the fits and starts and wild paths Jackie's conversations could take.

Justine was an old friend, a valued one. She was a woman he had always been completely at ease with. He knew her family, and she knew his. Their opinions might not always agree precisely, but they were invariably compatible. Over the ten years they'd known each other, they'd never become lovers. Justine's marriages and Nathan's travels had prevented that, though there had always been a light and companionable attraction between them.

That could change now, and they were both aware of it. She was single, and he was home. There would very likely never be a woman he knew better, a woman better suited to his tastes, than Justine Chesterfield.

He'd wanted, as he'd sat comfortably, to be back in his kitchen watching Jackie concoct a meal, even if the damn radio was playing.

He thought it entirely possible that he was losing his mind.

The evening had ended with a chaste, almost brotherly kiss. He hadn't wanted to make love with Justine, though God knew he was stirred up enough to need a woman. It infuriated him to realize that if he'd slept with Justine he would have thought of Jackie and felt like an adulterer.

There was no doubt about it. He was going crazy.

Giving up on trying to reason, even with himself, Nathan got out of the car. As he let himself in to the house he thought a long soak in the whirlpool might tire him out enough to let him sleep.

Jackie heard the movement downstairs and sat up in bed again. Nathan? She hadn't heard a car drive up and stop. She'd been listening for his return for over a half hour, and even in a half doze she would have heard. Crawling down to the foot of the bed, she strained to hear.

Silence.

If it was Nathan, why wasn't he coming upstairs? Annoyed because her heart was beginning to race, she crept to the door and peeked out.

If it was Nathan, why was he walking around in the dark?

Because it wasn't Nathan, she decided. It was a burglar who'd probably been watching the house for weeks, learning the routine and waiting for his chance. He'd know that she was alone in the house and asleep, so he'd broken in to rob Nathan blind.

With a hand to her heart, she glanced back toward her bed. She could call the police, then crawl under the covers. It sounded like a wonderful idea. Even as she took the first tiptoeing step back, she stopped.

But what if she hadn't really heard anything other than the house settling? If Nathan wasn't already fed up, he certainly would be if he got home from *that woman*'s and found the house full of police because she'd jumped the gun.

Taking a deep breath, Jackie decided to creep down and make sure there was a good reason to panic.

She descended the stairs slowly, keeping her back to the wall. Still no sound. The house was absolutely dark and absolutely silent. A burglar had to make some noise when he stole the family silver.

Probably just your imagination, she told herself as she reached the lower landing. In the dark she strained her ears but still heard nothing. As her heartbeat slowed to normal she decided to take one quick check around the house, knowing her imagination would play havoc if she went back to bed without satisfying her curiosity.

She began to whistle, just under her breath, as she moved from room to room. There was no one there, of course, but if there was, Jackie preferred to have them know she was on her way. Jackie's imagination, according to her mother, had always been bizarre.

By the time she'd wound through the living room, passed by Nathan's office and the powder room and gone into the dining area, she'd imagined not just your everyday intruder but a gang of psychotic thugs who'd recently escaped from a maximum-security prison in Kentucky. Determined to beat her own wayward fantasies, she stepped into the kitchen. Every light in the house blazed behind her. Now, as she reached for the switch in the kitchen, she heard a shuffle of footsteps.

Her fingers froze, but her mind didn't. They were in the sun room—at least six of them by now. One of them had a scar running from his temple to his jawline and had been serving time for bludgeoning senior citizens in their sleep. She took a step back, thinking of the phone in her room behind a locked door when the footsteps came closer.

Too late, her mind flashed. Going with impulse and desperation, she grabbed the closest weapon—the soufflé pan. Swinging it above her head, she prepared to defend herself.

When Nathan stepped into the room, dressed only in his briefs, it was a toss-up as to who was the more surprised. He jerked back, finding himself ridiculously embarrassed as Jackie let out a scream and dropped the pan. It landed with a resounding clatter just before she doubled over with hysterical giggles.

"What the hell are you doing, sneaking around the house?" If it wouldn't have made him feel that much more foolish, Nathan would have grabbed a dishcloth for cover.

Jackie slammed both hands over her mouth as she gasped and choked. "I thought you were six men with homicidal intentions. One of you had a scar, and the little one had a face like a weasel."

"So naturally you came down to beat us all off with a soufflé pan."

"Not exactly." Still giggling, she propped herself against the counter. "I'm sorry, I always laugh when I'm terrified."

"Who doesn't?"

"It was just that I thought there was a burglar, then I convinced myself there wasn't, and then..." She began to hiccup. "Then I thought you were this gang from Kentucky led by a man named Bubba. I need some water." Grabbing a glass, Jackie filled it to the rim while Nathan tried to follow.

"You've obviously picked the right field at last, Jack. With an imagination like that, you'll make a million."

"Thanks." Picking up the glass, she drank while running her finger in circles over the bottom.

"What the hell are you doing now?"

"Getting rid of the hiccups. Surefire." She set the glass down and waited. "See? All clear. Now it's your turn. What were you doing sneaking around the house in the dark in your underwear?"

"It's my house."

"Right you are. And it's very nice underwear, too. Sorry I scared you."

"You didn't scare me." Finding his temper once more on a short fuse, he bent down and scooped up the pan. "I was about to take a spa and decided I wanted a drink."

"Oh. Well, that explains that." Jackie pressed her lips together. It wouldn't do to start giggling again. "Did you have a nice time?"

"What? Yes, fine." This was a hell of a time, Nathan decided, to notice that she was wearing nothing but an oversize T-shirt with a faded picture of Mozart on the front. With care and effort, he kept his eyes on her face, but it didn't help very much. "I don't want to keep you up."

"Oh, that's okay. I'll fix you a drink."

"I can do it." He had his hand on her wrist before she could open the cupboard.

"No need to be cranky. I said I was sorry."

"I'm not cranky. Go to bed, Jack."

"I'm bothering you, aren't I?" she murmured as she turned to face him. With her free hand, she reached up to touch his cheek. "That's nice."

"Yes, you're bothering me, and it's not particularly nice." Her face was scrubbed free of cosmetics, but her scent still lingered. "Now go to bed."

"Want to come with me?"

His eyes narrowed at the smile in hers. "You're going to push too far."

"It was only a suggestion." She felt a wave of tenderness as she thought of how he would view his position and what was happening between them. An honorable man who thought his intentions were dishonorable. "Nathan, is it so hard for you to understand that I love you and want to make love with you?"

He didn't want it to make sense, couldn't allow it to make sense. "What's hard for me to understand and impossible for me to believe is that anyone could consider themselves in love after a matter of days. Things don't work that easily, Jack."

"Sometimes they do. Look at Romeo and Juliet. No, that's a bad example when you think of how things worked out." Fascinated by his mouth, warmed by the memory of how it felt on hers, she traced it with her fingertip. "Sorry, I guess I can't think of a good example right now because I'm thinking about you."

His stomach wound itself into a tight knot. "If you're trying to make this difficult, you're succeeding."

"Impossible was the idea, but I'll settle for difficult." She shifted closer. Their thighs brushed. Her eyelids lowered. "Kiss me, Nathan. Even my imagination falls short of what it's like when you do."

He swore at her, or tried to, but his mouth was already against hers. Each time it was a little sweeter, a little sharper, a little more difficult to forget. He was losing, and he knew it. Once he gave in to his own needs, he wasn't sure he'd be able to pull back. Nor did he know precisely what he would find himself trapped in.

She was a drug to a man who had always been obsessively clear-minded, a slide down a cliff to one who had always been firmly sure-footed.

And she was naked beneath that loose shirt. Soft and naked and already warm for him. He found himself reaching, testing, taking, even as warning bells rang inside his head.

DANGER. PROCEED AT YOUR OWN RISK.

His own risk. He'd always carefully calculated the risk, the odds, the degrees and angles, before he took the first step. Her body seemed to have been molded for his hands, for his pleasure, for his needs. There was no way to calculate this, or her, or what happened every time they touched each other.

It was so easy, so mindlessly easy, to take the next step. Blindly, recklessly. She was murmuring his name as her hands glided up his back, then down to his hips. He could feel every curve and angle of her body as his hands moved over and under the thin cotton. How could it be so familiar yet so fresh, so comforting yet so unnerving?

He wanted to scoop her up, to wallow in her, to lose himself. It would have been so easy. Her body was poised against his, ready, waiting, eager. And the heat, the heat he'd begun to recognize and expect, was weighing down on his brain. There was nothing and no one he'd ever wanted more.

Somewhere in the back of his mind he heard a door slam and a key turn in a lock. In a last attempt at self-defense, he pulled her away.

"Hold it."

Sighing, half dreaming, she opened her eyes. "Hmmm?"

If she kept looking at him like that he was going to fall apart. Or rip that excuse for nightgear off her back. "Look, I don't know why this is happening, but it has to stop. I'm not hypocrite enough to say I don't want you, but I'm not crazy enough to start something that's going to make us both miserable."

"Why should making love make either of us miserable?"

"Because it could never go beyond that." Because she swayed toward him, he put his hands on her shoulders. Damn it, she was trembling. Or he was. "I don't have room for you, for anyone, in my life, Jack. I don't want to make room. I don't think you understand that."

"No, I don't." She leaned forward to brush her lips over his chin. "If I believed it, I'd think it was very sad."

"Believe it." But he was no longer certain he did. "My work comes first. It takes all my time, my energy and my concentration. That's the way I want it. A blistering affair with you has its appeal, but . . . for some reason I care about you, and I don't think that's all you want or need."

"It doesn't have to be all."

"But it does, and that's something for you to think about." He had to stay calm now, calm enough to make her listen. "In six weeks I go to Denver. When I've finished there, it's Sydney. After that I don't know where I'll be or for how long. I travel light, and that doesn't include a lover, or the worry about someone waiting for me back home."

She shook her head as she took a small step back. "I wonder what happened to make you so unwilling to share yourself, so determined to keep to some straight-and-narrow path. No curves, no detours, Nathan?" She tilted her head to study him. There was no anger in her eyes, just a sympathy he didn't want. "It's more than sad, it's sinful, really, to turn away someone who loves you because you don't want to spoil your routine."

He opened his mouth so that the words nearly tumbled out. Reasons, explanations, an anger he barely remembered or thought he'd forgotten. Years of control snapped into place.

"Maybe it is, but that's the way I live. The way I've chosen to live." He'd hurt her again, badly this time. The shiver of pain sliced back at him, and he knew he was hurting himself, as well. "I can tell you that if you were another woman it would be a lot easier to turn away. I don't want to feel what I'm feeling for you. Do you understand?"

"Yes. I wish I didn't." She looked down at the floor. When her eyes lifted again, the hurt was still there, but it had been joined by a flash of something stronger. "What you don't understand is that I don't give up. Blame it on the Irish. A stubborn breed. I want you, Nathan, and no matter how far you run or how fast, I'll catch up. When I do, all your neat little plans are going to tumble like a stack of dominoes." Taking his face in her hands, she kissed him hard. "And you'll thank me for it, because no one's ever going to love you the way I do."

She kissed him again, more gently this time, then turned away. "I made some fresh lemonade, if you still want a drink. Night."

He watched her go with the sinking feeling that he could already hear the clatter of dominoes.

Chapter Seven

She should have hated him. Sarah wanted to, wished the strong, destructive emotions would come, filling all the cracks in her feelings, blocking out everything else. With hate, a coolheaded, sharply honed hate, she would have felt in control again. She needed badly to feel in control again. But she didn't hate him. Couldn't.

Even knowing Jake had spent the night with another woman, kissing another woman's lips, touching another woman's skin, she couldn't hate him. But she could grieve for the loss, for the death of a beauty that had never had the chance to bloom fully.

She had come to understand what they might have had together. She had nearly come to accept that they belonged together, whatever their differences, whatever the risks. He would always live by his gun and by his own set of rules, but with her, briefly, perhaps reluctantly, he had shown such kindness, such tenderness.

There was a place for her in his heart. Sarah knew it. Beneath the rough-hewn exterior was a man who believed in justice, who was capable of small, endearing kindnesses. He'd allowed her to see that part of him, a part she knew he'd shared with few others.

Then why, the moment she had begun to soften toward him, to accept him for what and who he was, had he turned to another woman, a woman of easy virtue?

A woman of easy virtue? Jackie said to herself, and rolled her eyes. If that was the best she could come up with, she'd better hang it up right now.

It hadn't been one of her better days. Nathan had been up and gone before she'd started breakfast. He'd left her a note—she couldn't even say a scribbled note, because his handwriting was as disciplined as the rest of him—telling her he'd be out most of the day.

She'd munched on a candy bar and the last of the ginger ale as she'd mulled over the current situation. As far as she could see, it stank.

She was in love with a man who was determined to hold her, and his own feelings, at arm's length. A man who insisted on rationalizing those feelings away—not because he was committed to another woman, not because he was suffering from a fatal disease, not because he was hiding a criminal past, but because they were inconvenient.

He was too honorable to take advantage of the situation, and too stubborn to admit that he and she belonged together.

No room in his life for her? Jackie thought as she pushed away from the typewriter and began to pace. Did he really believe she would take a ridiculous statement like that and back off? Of course she wouldn't, but what bothered her more was that he would make a statement like that in the first place.

What made him so determined not to accept love when it was given, so determined not to acknowledge his own emotions? Her own family could sometimes be annoyingly proper, but there had always been a wealth of love generously given. She'd grown up unafraid of feelings. If you didn't feel, you weren't alive, so what was the purpose? She knew Nathan felt, and felt deeply, but whenever his emotions took control he stepped back and put up those walls.

He did love her, Jackie thought as she flopped down on the bed. She couldn't be mistaken about that. But he was going to fight her every inch of the way. So she'd handle it. It wasn't that she objected to a good fight, it was just that this one hurt. Every time he drew back, every time he denied what they had together, it hurt a little more.

She'd been honest with him, and that hadn't worked. She'd been deliberately provocative, and that hadn't done so well, either. She'd been annoying, and she'd been cooperative. She wasn't sure what step to take next.

Rolling onto her stomach, she debated the idea of taking a nap. It was midafternoon, she'd worked nonstop since breakfast, and she couldn't drum up any enthusiasm for the pool. Perhaps if she went to sleep with Nathan on her mind she would wake up with a solution. Deciding to trust the Fates—after all, they'd gotten her this far—she closed her eyes. She'd nearly dozed off when the doorbell rang.

Someone selling encyclopedias, she thought groggily, with the idea of ignoring them. Or it was three men in white suits passing out pamphlets for a tent revival—which actually might be fairly interesting. With a yawn, she snuggled into the pillow. She'd nearly shut off her mind when a last thought intruded. It was a telegram from home, and someone had been in a horrible accident.

Springing up, she sprinted downstairs.

"Yes, I'm coming!" As she pushed the hair out of her eyes, she yanked the door open.

It wasn't a telegram or a door-to-door salesman. It was Justine Chesterfield. Jackie decided it really wasn't one of her better days. She leaned on the door and offered a chilly smile.

"Hello."

"Hello. I wonder if Nathan might be around."

"Sorry, he's out." Her fingers on the knob itched to close the door quietly and completely. That would be rude. Jackie could almost hear her mother upbraiding her. She took a long breath before moderating her tone. "He didn't say where he was going or when he'd be back, but you're welcome to wait if you'd like."

"Thanks." They exchanged appraising glances before Justine stepped over the threshold.

The woman's dressed as if she's just stepped off a yacht, Jackie thought nastily. In Hyannis Port. At the beginning of the season. Justine's tall, softly curved body was set off nicely by white slacks and a boat-necked silk T-shirt in crimson. She'd added a quietly elegant necklace of twisted gold links and discreetly stylish matching earrings. Her hair had been left down to wave gently on her shoulders, scooped back at the temples by two mother-of-pearl combs.

She was perfect. Perfectly lovely, perfectly groomed, perfectly mannerly. Jackie was glad she could hate her.

"I hope I'm not disturbing you...." Justine began.

"Not at all." Jackie gestured toward the living room. "Make yourself at home."

"Thanks." Justine wandered in, then set her envelope bag on a small table. The bag matched her open-toed white snakeskin pumps. "You must be Jacqueline, Fred's cousin."

"I must be."

"I'm Justine Chesterfield. An old friend of Nathan's."

"I recognized your voice." Ingrained manners had Jackie offering a hand. As their fingers touched briefly, a smile hovered around Justine's mouth. Unfortunately for Jackie, the smile was friendly and entirely too appealing.

"And I yours. According to Nathan, Fred's as devious as he is charming."

"More so, believe me." So this was the kind of woman Nathan preferred. Quietly polished, quietly stylish, quietly stunning. Trying not to sigh, Jackie played hostess. "Can I get you something? A cold drink, some coffee?"

"I'd love something cold, if you wouldn't mind."

"All right, have a seat. I'll just be a minute."

Jackie muttered to herself the entire time she fixed lemonade and arranged shortbread cookies on Nathan's depression-glass platter. It rarely occurred to her to think how she looked when she planned on staying in. But she would have picked today to wear her most comfortable and most ragged pair of cutoffs, with a baggy athletic-style T-shirt in garish green-and-yellow stripes. There was a small fortune in gold and gems on her fingers, and her feet were bare. The Sizzling Cerise on her toes had begun to chip.

The hell with that, she thought, and made one vague and futile attempt to finger-comb her hair. She'd let Ms. Sleek-and-Stylish have her say.

She was sure that Sarah would have been just as gracious to Carlotta, but she had a feeling that Sarah was a much nicer person than Jacqueline R. MacNamara. Determined to give Nathan nothing to snarl about, she lifted the tray and started back to her guest. Nathan's guest.

The sunlight and the strong masculine colors of the room were certainly flattering to Justine. It didn't help to admit it, but Jackie was nothing if not honest.

"This is awfully nice of you," Justine began as she took a seat. "Actually, I was hoping we'd have a chance to talk. Are you very busy? Nathan told me you were working on a book."

"He did?" It was surprise more than a desire to chat that had Jackie sitting. She hadn't thought Nathan even remembered she was writing, much less that he would tell someone else about it. And Justine was the second person, after Mrs. Grange, who hadn't smirked when she'd spoken of her writing.

"Yes, he said you were writing a novel and that you were very dedicated and disciplined about your work. Nathan's a big believer in discipline."

"So I've noticed." Jackie discovered she didn't mind sipping a glass of lemonade after all. Justine had just handed her the perfect route to make her excuses and disappear back upstairs. After a second sip, Jackie decided to tour around it. "As it turns out, I was just taking a break when you rang the bell."

"That's lucky." Justine chose a cookie and nibbled. Her scent was very sophisticated, not opulent but rich and feminine. Jackie noticed that her nails were long, rounded and painted a pale rose. She wore only one ring, a stunning opal surrounded by diamonds. "I suppose I should apologize first."

Jackie left off her study long enough to lift a brow. "Apologize?"

"For the mix-up here between you and Nathan." Justine noticed with a little stab of envy that Jackie's skin was free of cosmetics and as clear as spring-water. "It was I who talked Nathan into letting Fred move in while he was away in Europe. It seemed like such a perfect solution at the time, as Nathan was concerned about leaving his house empty for that length of time and Fred seemed to be at loose ends."

"Fred's always at loose ends," Jackie said over the rim of her glass. She looked at Justine with a trace of sympathy. Fred's charm might not have swayed Mrs. Grange, but the housekeeper was the exception to the rule. "He also has a way of making you believe he can spin straw into gold. As long as you're paying for the straw."

"So I understand." Appreciation for the analogy showed in Justine's eyes. "I feel, well . . . a little guilty that Fred absconded with your money under false pretenses."

"No need." Jackie took a healthy bite out of a cookie. "I've known Fred all my life. If anyone should have seen through him, I should have. In any case," she added with what she thought was a wonderfully cool smile, "Nathan and I have come to a satisfactory arrangement."

"So he said." Justine took another sip of lemonade, watching Jackie over the rim. "Apparently you're a first-class cook."

"Yes." She didn't believe in denying the truth, but she wondered what else Nathan had felt obligated to tell Justine. If they were going to fight, she thought restlessly, why didn't they just get on with it?

"I've never been able to put two ingredients together and have either one come out recognizable. Did you really study in Paris?"

"Which time?" Despite herself, Jackie smiled. She hadn't wanted to like Justine. True, the woman was very cool and very polished, but there was something kind in her eyes. Kindness, no matter what the package, always drew her in.

Justine smiled in return, and the restraint between them lowered by another few degrees. "Miss Mac-Namara—Jacqueline—may I be frank?"

"Things usually get done faster that way."

"You're not at all what I expected."

Jackie sat back, tucking up her legs Indian-style. "What did you expect?"

"I always thought when Nathan became besotted about someone she'd be very sleek and self-contained. Possibly boring."

The lemonade that was halfway down Jackie's throat had to be swallowed in a hard gulp. "Back up. Did you say Nathan was besotted?"

"A wreck. Didn't you know?"

"He hides it well," Jackie murmured.

"Well, it was perfectly obvious to me last night." The heat in Jackie's eyes came instantly and automatically. "We've never been anything but friends, by the way." Justine gave a small shrug. "If I were in your position, I'd appreciate someone making that clear to me."

The heat simmered a moment longer, then snuffed itself out. She didn't often feel like a fool, but she was willing to accept it when she did. "I do appreciate it— your telling me, and the fact that you've never been anything but friends. Would you mind if I asked you why?"

"I've wondered myself." With the ease of a woman who never gained an ounce, Justine took another cookie. "The timing's never been quite right. I'm not independent." This was said with another shrug. "I enjoy being married, being part of a couple, so I end up doing it quite a bit. I was married when I met Nathan. Then, after my first divorce, we were in different parts of the country. It's continued to work out about the same way for close to a decade. In any case, it's enough to say that I was always involved with someone else and Nathan was always involved with his work. For his own reasons, he prefers things that way."

Jackie wanted to ask why, suspected that Justine might have some of the answers. But she couldn't go that far. If what she had with Nathan was going to work, the explanations would have to come from him. "I appreciate you telling me. I suppose I should tell you that you're not what I expected, either."

"And what did you expect?"

"A calculating adventuress with icicles on her heart and designs on my man. I spent most of last night detesting you." When Justine's lips curved at the description, Jackie was very glad she'd refrained from giving Carlotta that wart.

"Then I wasn't wrong in thinking you care about Nathan?"

"I'm in love with him."

Justine smiled again. There was a trace of wistfulness in it that told Jackie more than words could have. "He needs someone. He doesn't think so, but he does."

"I know. And it's going to be me."

"Then I'll wish you luck. I didn't intend to when I came."

"What changed your mind?"

"You invited me in and offered me a drink when you wished me to hell."

Jackie grinned. "And I thought I was so discreet."

"No, you weren't. Jack...that's what Nathan calls you, isn't it?"

"Most of the time."

"Jack, my track record with relationships isn't what you would call impressive—in fact, let's continue to be frank and admit it's lousy—but I'd like to offer you a little advice."

"I'll take anything I can get."

"Some men need more of a push than others. Use both hands with Nathan."

"I intend to." With her head tilted to one side, Jackie considered. "You know, Justine, I have this cousin. Second cousin on my father's side. Not Fred," she said quickly. "This one's a college professor at the University of Michigan. Do you like the intellectual type?"

With a laugh, Justine set down her glass. "Ask me again in six months. I'm on sabbatical."

When Nathan arrived home a few hours later, he knew nothing of Justine's visit or of the conclusions that had been reached in his living room. Perhaps that was for the best.

It was bad enough that he was glad to be home. It was a different sort of glad from the feeling he'd had when he'd arrived from Germany. Then he'd been looking forward to the familiar, to solitude, to the routine he had set for himself over the years. He didn't—wouldn't have—considered it stuffy, just convenient.

Now a part of him, a part he still wasn't ready to acknowledge, was glad to come home to Jackie. There was an anticipation, a surge of excitement at knowing she was there to talk with, to relax with, even to spar with. The unfamiliar, and the companionship, added a new dimension to an evening at home. The challenge of outmaneuvering her had become a habit he hadn't been aware of forming. Somewhere along the

line he'd stopped resenting the fact that she'd invaded
his privacy.

He heard the music the moment he opened the door.
It wasn't the rock he'd grown accustomed to hearing
from the kitchen but one of Strauss's lovely and sen-
sual waltzes. Though he wasn't sure if her change in
radio stations was something to worry about, he was
cautious as he slipped into his office to put away his
briefcase and the reinforced tubes that held the blueprints from his project in Denver.

Loosening his tie, he started into the kitchen. As
usual, something smelled wonderful.

She wasn't wearing her habitual shorts. Instead, she
wore a jumpsuit in some soft, silky material the color
of melted butter. It didn't cling to her body so much
as shift around it, offering hints. Her feet were bare,
and she wore one long wooden earring. She was busy
slicing a round loaf of crusty bread. He had a sudden
feeling, strong and lucid, that he should turn and run,
as fast and as far as he could. Because it annoyed him,
Nathan stepped through the archway.

"Hello, Jack."

She'd known he was there, but she managed to look
mildly and credibly surprised when she turned. "Hi."
He looked so attractive in a suit, with the knot of his
tie pulled loose. Because her heart turned to mush, she
walked over and kissed his cheek. "How was your
day?"

He didn't know what to make of her. So what else
was new? But he did know that her casual greeting kiss
was exactly what he'd needed, and it worried him.
"Busy," he told her.

"Well, you'll have to tell me all about it, but you should have some wine first." She was already pouring two glasses. The sun hit the liquid as it rushed into the crystal and shot it through with gold. "I hope you're hungry. It'll be ready in just a couple minutes."

He accepted the wine and didn't ask why her timing always seemed so perfect. It made him wonder if she'd managed to slip a homing device on him. "Did you get much done today?"

"Quite a bit." Jackie began to arrange the bread she'd sliced in a basket. "I had a little lull this afternoon, but things really picked up afterward." Her lips curved as she lifted her wine, and once again he had the feeling that there was something he should know, but he didn't want to ask. "I've decided to concentrate on the first hundred pages for the next week or so, until it's ready to send off to an agent I know in New York."

"That's good," he managed, wondering why the idea sent him into a panic. He wanted her to progress, didn't he? The more she did, the less guilty he'd feel about telling her that her time was up. No amount of logic could erase the niggling fear that she would tell him she no longer needed the house to work in and was moving on. "It must be going well."

"Better than I expected, and I always expect quite a lot." The timer buzzed, and she turned to the oven. Fortunately, the move hid her smile. "I thought we'd eat on the patio. It's such a nice evening."

The warning bells sounded again, but they were dimmer and less urgent. "It's going to rain."

"Not for a couple of hours yet." With her hands buried in oven mitts, she drew out a casserole. "I hope you like this. It's called *schinkenfleckerln*." Jackie whipped out the foreign name like a native.

There was something very homey and nonthreatening about the pot of browned noodles and ham in bubbling sauce. "It looks terrific."

"A very simple Austrian recipe," she told him. That explained the Viennese waltz, he thought. "Grab the bread, will you? I've already set up outside."

Again, she timed it perfectly. The sun was dropping in the sky. The clouds that were gathering to bring rain during the night were tipped with pink and orange. The air was cool, with a catchy breeze from the east that brought just a hint of the sea.

The round patio table was set for two. Informally. Nathan would have to have stretched a point to call it deliberately romantic. Colorful mats she must have bought herself were under his white everyday dishes. She'd added flowers, but they were only a few sprigs of daisies in a colored bottle. The bottle wasn't his, either, so he could only suppose that she'd been foraging in some of the local shops.

He settled back as Jackie began the business of serving. "I haven't thanked you for all the meals."

She only smiled as she sat across from him. "That was the deal."

"I know, but you've gone to more trouble than you had to. I appreciate it."

"That's nice. I really like to cook when there's someone to share it with. Nothing more depressing than cooking for one."

He hadn't thought so. Once. "Jack..." She looked up at him, her eyes big and round and soft, and he lost track of what he'd planned to say. Groping, he picked up his wine. "I, ah...I feel like we got off on the wrong foot. Since we're both victims, so to speak, I'd like to call a truce."

"I thought we had."

"An official one."

"All right." She lifted her glass and tapped it against his. "Live long and prosper."

"I beg your pardon?"

Jackie chuckled into her wine. "I should have known you wouldn't be a fan of *Star Trek*. That's the Vulcan greeting, Nathan, but to keep it simple, I'll just wish you the best."

"Thanks." Unconsciously he loosened his tie a little more. "Why don't you tell me about your book?"

It was a first, Nathan decided, to see Jackie speechless. Her lips parted, not to smile or to toss a quip, but in utter surprise. "Really?" she managed after a moment.

"Yes, I'd like to hear what it's about." He picked up a hunk of bread and began to butter it. "Don't you want to talk about it?"

"Well, yes, it's just that I didn't think you were interested. You never asked, or even commented, and I know that I usually beat people over the head with whatever I'm doing at the time because I get too involved and lose perspective. So I thought it would be better if I just kept the book to myself since I was already driving you crazy. I figured under the circumstances, counting Fred and six months in Frankfurt, you'd probably hate it anyway."

Nathan scooped up some of the casserole, chewed and considered. "I understand that," he said. "I can't tell you how much that terrifies me, but I understand. Now, why don't you tell me about your book?"

"Okay." She moistened her lips. "I've set it in what is now Arizona, in the 1870s—a decade or so after the Mexican War, when it was ceded to the U.S. as part of New Mexico. I'd toyed around with doing a generational thing and starting in the eighteenth century, when it was still a European settlement, but I found that I wanted to get into the meat right away."

"No meat in the eighteenth century?"

"Oh, pounds of it." She took a piece of bread herself and shredded it before she realized she was nervous. "But Jake and Sarah weren't alive then. My protagonists," Jackie explained. "It's really their story, and I was too impatient to start the book a hundred years before they came along. He's a gunfighter and she's convent-bred. I liked the idea of putting them in Arizona because it really epitomizes America's Old West. The Earps, the Claytons, Tombstone, Tucson, Apaches." Nerves disappeared as she began to imagine. "It gives it that nice bloody frontier tradition."

"Shoot-outs, bounty hunters and Indian raids?"

"That's the idea. The setup has Sarah coming West after her father dies. He, Sarah's father, had led her to believe that he's a prosperous miner. She's grown up in the East, learning all the things that well-bred young ladies of good familes are supposed to learn. Then, after his sudden death, she comes out to the Arizona Territory and discovers that for all the years she was living in moderate luxury back East, her father had barely been scraping by on this dilapidated gold mine, spending every penny he could spare on her education."

"Now she's penniless, orphaned and out of her element."

"Exactly." Pleased with him, Jackie poured more wine. "I figure that makes her instantly vulnerable and sympathetic, as well as plunging her into immediate jeopardy. Anyway, it doesn't take her long to discover that her father didn't die in an accidental cave-in, but was murdered. By this time, she's already had a few run-ins with Jake Redman, the hard-bitten gun-for-hire renegade who stands for everything she's been taught to detest. He saved her life during an Apache raid."

"So he's not all bad."

"A diamond in the rough," Jackie explained over a bite of bread. "See, there were a lot of miners and adventurers in the territory during this period, but the War Between the States and troop withdrawal were delaying settlement, so the Apaches were still dominant. That made it a very wild and dangerous place for a gently bred young woman to be."

"But she stays."

"If she'd turned to run, she'd have been pitiful rather than sympathetic. Big difference. She's compelled to discover who killed her father and why. Then there's the fact that she's desperately, though unwillingly, attracted to Jake Redman."

"And he to her?"

"You've got it." She smiled at him as she toyed with her wine. "You see, Jake, like a lot of men—and women, for that matter—doesn't believe he needs anyone, certainly not someone who would interfere with his life-style and convince him to settle down. He's a loner, has always been a loner, and intends to keep it that way.''

His brow lifted as he sipped. ''Very clever,'' he said mildly.

Pleased that he saw the correlation, she smiled. ''Yes, I thought so. But Sarah's quite determined. Once she discovers that she loves him, that her life would never be complete without him, she wears him down. Of course, Carlotta does her best to botch things up.''

''Carlotta?''

''The town's leading woman of ill repute. It's not so much that she wants Jake, though of course she does. They all do. But she hates Sarah and everything Sarah stands for. Then there's the fact that she knows Sarah's father had been murdered because, after five years, he'd finally hit the mother lode. The mine Sarah now holds the claim for is worth a fortune. That's as far as I've gotten.''

''But how does it end?''

''I don't know.''

''What do you mean, you don't know? You're writing it, you have to know.''

''No, I don't. In fact, I'm almost certain if I knew, exactly, it wouldn't be half as much fun to sit down every day.'' She offered him more of the casserole, but he shook his head. ''It's a story for me, too, and I am getting closer, but it's not like a blueprint, Nathan.''

Because she could see he didn't understand, she leaned closer, elbows propped on the table. ''I'll tell you why I think I'd never have made a good architect, though I found the whole process fascinating and the idea of taking an empty lot and bringing it alive with a building incredible.''

He glanced over again at that. What she'd said, and how she'd phrased it, encompassed his own feelings so perfectly that he could almost believe she'd stepped into his mind.

"You have to know every detail, beginning to end. You have to be certain before you take out the first shovel of dirt how it's going to end up. When you build, you're not just responsible for creating an attractive, functional piece of work. You're also responsible for the lives of the people who will work or live in or pass through the building, climb the stairs, ride the elevators. Nothing can be left to chance, and imagination has to conform to safety and practicality.''

"I think you're wrong," he said after a moment. "I think you'd have made an excellent architect.''

She smiled at him. "No, just because I understand doesn't mean I can do. Believe me, I've been there.'' She touched his hand easily, friend to friend. "You're an excellent architect because not only do you understand, but you're able to combine art with practicality, creativity with reality.''

He studied her, both moved and pleased by her insight. "Is that what you're doing with your writing?''

"I hope so.'' She sat back to watch the clouds roll in. It would rain soon after nightfall. "All my life I've been scrambling around, looking for one creative outlet after another. Music, painting, dancing. I composed my first sonata when I was ten.'' Her lips tilted in a self-deprecating grin. "I was precocious.''

"No, really?"

She chuckled as she slipped her hand under the bowl of her glass. "It wasn't a particularly good sonata, but I always knew there was something I had to do. My parents have been very patient, even indulgent, and I didn't always deserve it. This time...I guess this sounds silly at my age, but this time I want them to be proud of me."

"It doesn't sound silly," he murmured. "We never grow out of wanting our parents' approval."

"Do you have yours, Nathan?"

"Yes." The word was clipped. Because he heard it himself, he added a smile. "They're both very pleased with the route my career's taken."

She decided to press just a little farther. "Your father isn't an architect, is he?"

"No. Finance."

"Ah. That's funny, when you think of it. I imagine our parents have had cocktails together more than once. J.D.'s biggest interests are in finance."

"You call your father J.D.?"

"Only when I'm thinking of him as a businessman. He'd always get such a kick out of it when I'd march into his office, plop on his desk and say, 'All right, J.D., is it buy or sell?'"

"You're very fond of him."

"I'm crazy about him. Mother, too, even when she nags. She's always wanting me to fly to Paris and be redone." With only the faintest of frowns, she touched the tips of her hair. "She's certain the French could find a way to make me elegant and demure."

"I like you the way you are."

Again he saw that quick look of astonishment on her face. "That's the nicest thing you've ever said to me."

He thought, as he stared into her eyes, that he heard the first rumble of thunder. "We'd better get this stuff inside. Rain's coming."

"All right." She rose easily enough and helped clear the table. It was foolish to be moved by such a simple statement. He hadn't told her she was beautiful or brilliant. He hadn't said he loved her madly. He'd simply told her that he liked her the way she was. Nothing he could have said would have meant more to a woman like Jackie.

Inside the kitchen, they worked together for a few moments in companionable silence.

"I suppose," she began, "since you're dressed like that, you didn't spend the day at the beach."

"No, I had meetings. My clients from Denver."

Jackie looked at what was left in the wine bottle, decided it wasn't enough to cork and poured the remainder into their glasses. "You never mentioned what you were going to build."

"S and S Industries is putting a branch in Denver. They need an office building."

"You designed another one of them in Dallas a few years ago."

Surprised, he glanced over. "Yes, I did."

"Is this one going to be along the same lines?"

"No. I went for slick and futuristic in Dallas. Lots of glass and steel, with an uncluttered look. I want something more classic for this. Softer, more distinguished lines."

"Can I see the drawings?"

"I suppose, if you'd like."

"I really would." She dried her hands on a cloth, then handed him his half-filled glass. "Can I see them now?"

"All right." He didn't question the fact that he wanted her to see them, that her opinion mattered to him. Both were new concepts for him, and something to think about later. They walked through the house as the light grew dim from the gathering clouds.

His desk was clear. Nathan would never have gone to a meeting without dealing with any leftover paperwork or correspondence. Drawing the blueprints from the tube, he spread them out. Genuinely interested, Jackie leaned over his shoulder with her lips pursed.

"The exterior is brown brick," he began, trying to ignore the brush of her hair against his cheek as she leaned closer. "I'm using curves rather than straight lines."

"It has a deco look."

"Exactly." Why hadn't he noticed her scent earlier? Was he just growing accustomed to it, or was it because she was standing so close, close enough to touch or to taste with the slightest effort? "I've arched the windows, and..."

When he let his words trail off, she glanced up and smiled. Understanding and patience shouldn't make a man uncomfortable, but he looked back deliberately at the papers on his desk.

"And every individual office will have at least one. I've always felt that it's more conducive to productivity if you don't feel caged in."

"Yes." She was still smiling, and neither of them were looking at the blueprints. "It's a beautiful building, very strong without being oppressive. Classic without being staid. The trim and accents are in rose, I imagine."

"To blend with the bricks." Her mouth was rose, a very soft, very subtle rose. He found himself turning his head just enough to taste it.

This time he knew he heard thunder, and it was much closer.

He drew away, shaken. Without speaking, he began to roll up the blueprints.

"I'd like to see the sketches of the interior."

"Jack—"

"It's not really fair to leave things half done."

Nodding, Nathan unrolled the next set. She was right. He supposed he'd known that all along. A thing begun required a finish.

Chapter Eight

Jackie drew a long, steadying breath. She felt like a diver who'd just taken the last bounce on the board. There could be no turning back now.

She hadn't known when she'd started the evening that he would allow her to get this close. The defenses he had were lowering, and the distance he insisted on was narrowing. It was difficult, very difficult, to accept that the reason for that might only be his own desire. But if that was all he could feel for her now, that was all she would ask for. Desire, at least, was honest.

She couldn't love him any more than she already did. That was what she had thought, but now she knew it wasn't true. With every step closer, with every hour spent with him, her heart expanded.

Patient, even sympathetic to his dilemma, she listened while he explained the floor plans.

It was an excellent piece of work. Her eye and her knowledge were sharp enough to recognize that. But so was he. An excellent piece of work. His hands were wide palmed and long fingered, tanned from the hours he spent outdoors watching over his projects, artistic in their own competent, no-nonsense way. His voice was strong, masculine without being gruff, cultured without being affected. There was a trace of lime scent on his skin from his soap.

She murmured in agreement and put a hand on his arm as he pointed out a facet of the building. There were muscles beneath the creaseless material of his tailored, conservative suit. She heard his voice hesitate at her touch. And she, too, heard the thunder.

"There'll be an atrium here, in the executive offices. We're going to use tile rather than carpet for a cooler, cleaner look. And here..." His mouth was drying up on the words, his muscles tightening at her casual touch. He found it necessary to sit.

"The boardroom?" Jackie prompted, and sat on the arm of his chair.

"What? Yes." His tie was strangling him. Nathan tugged at it and struggled to concentrate. "We'll continue with the arches, but on a larger scale. The paneling will—" He wondered why in the hell the paneling had ever mattered. Her hand was on his shoulder now, kneading away the tension he hadn't even been aware had lodged there.

"What about the paneling?"

What about it? he thought as she leaned forward to trail one of her slender, ringed fingers over the prints. "We're going with mahogany. Honduras."

"It'll be beautiful. Now, and a hundred years from now. Indirect lighting?"

"Yes." He looked at her again. She was smiling, her head tilted just inches above his, her body curved just slightly toward him. The ink on the blueprint of his life seemed to fade. "Jack, this can't go on."

"I agree completely." In one lithe move, she was in his lap.

"What are you doing?" It shouldn't have amused him. His stomach had just contracted into a fist, one with claws, but he found himself smiling at her.

"You're right, this can't go on. I'm sure you're going as crazy as I am, and we can't have that, can we?" A trio of rings glittered on her hand as she tucked her hair back.

"I suppose not."

"No. So I'm going to put a stop to it."

"To what?" He put a hand on her wrist as she slipped off his tie.

"To the uncertainty, to the what-ifs." Ignoring his hand, she began to unbutton his shirt. "This is very nice material," she commented. "I'm taking full responsibility, Nathan. You really have no say in the matter."

"What are you talking about, Jack?" He took her by the shoulders when she started to peel off his jacket. "What the hell do you think you're doing?"

"I'm having my way with you, Nathan." She pressed her mouth to his, and the laugh he'd thought he was ready to form became a moan. "It's no use trying to fight it, you know," she murmured against his lips as she pulled off his jacket. "I'm a very determined woman."

"So I see." He felt her tug at his shirt from the waistband of his slacks and tried again. "Jack—damn it, Jackie, we'd better talk about this."

"No more talk." She nipped lightly at his collarbone, then slid her tongue to his ear. "I'm going to have you, Nathan, willing or not." She closed her teeth over his earlobe. "Don't make me hurt you."

This time he did laugh, though not steadily. "Jack, I outweigh you by seventy pounds."

"The bigger they are..." she told him, and unhooked his slacks. In an automatic defensive gesture, his hands covered hers.

"You're serious."

She drew back far enough to look at him just as the first slice of lightning lit the sky. The flash leaped into her eyes as if it had always been there, waiting. "Deadly." With her eyes on his, she caught the zipper of her jumpsuit between her thumb and fingers and drew it down. "You're not getting out of this room until I'm finished with you, Nathan. Cooperate, and I'll be gentle. Otherwise..." She shrugged, and the jumpsuit slithered tantalizingly down her shoulders.

It was too late, much too late, to pretend he didn't want to be with her, didn't have to be with her. The game she was playing was taking the responsibility and the repercussions away from him and onto her. Though it touched him, he couldn't allow it.

"I want you." He brushed her cheeks with his hands and combed his fingers through her hair as he said it. "Come upstairs."

She turned her face so that her lips pressed into his palm. It was a gesture of great tenderness, a gesture that bordered on submission. But when she looked back at him, she shook her head. "Right here. Right now." Jackie pressed her open mouth to his, leaving him no choice.

She tantalized, tormented, teased. Her body curled itself around his, and her lips were quick and urgent. They lingered on his, drawing in, drawing out, then sped away to trace the planes and angles of his face. His blood was hammering. He could feel it, in his head, in his loins, in his fingertips. Her hands were unmerciful...wonderful...as they roamed over him.

No hesitation. She didn't know the meaning of the word. Like the storm that whipped at the windows, she was all flash and fire. A man could get burned by her, he thought, and always bear the scars. Yet his arms banded around her, holding her hard and close as he fought to maintain some control. She was driving him beyond the limits he'd always set for himself, away from reason, away from the civilized.

That was his own breath he heard, fast and uneven. That was his skin springing moist and hot from a need that had grown titanic in mere moments. He was pulling the material from her shoulders with a gnawing demand to feel her flesh against his. And it was with an insatiable greed that he took it.

"Jack." His mouth was against her throat as he tasted, devoured. More...he could only think of having more. He'd have absorbed her into him if he'd known how. "Jack," he repeated. "Give me a minute, will you?"

But her mouth was just as greedy when it came to his. She only laughed.

He swore, but even the oath caught in his throat. He was tearing the jumpsuit from her as they slid to the floor.

She couldn't make her fingers work fast enough. Jackie pulled and yanked to strip the last barriers of his clothing away. She wanted to feel him, all of him. As they rolled over on the carpet, her skin was on fire from the friction of flesh against flesh.

She'd thought she would guide him, coerce, cajole, seduce. She'd been wrong. Like a pebble in a slingshot, she'd been flung high and fast, no longer in control. But with some trace of reason, she knew he was as lost as she.

Desire held control, steered by a love only one of them could admit. But in the lamplight, with the storm reaching its peak, desire was enough.

Wrapped together, they rolled mindlessly, each searching and finding more. The capacity for intense concentration was inherent in them both, but neither had used it so fully in the act of love until tonight. The clothes they'd discarded tangled with their naked legs and were kicked heedlessly away. Rain, tossed by a restless wind, hit the windows like bullets but was ignored. Something teetered on a table as it was jolted, then thudded to the carpet. Neither of them heard.

There were no murmured promises, no whispered endearments. Only sighs and shudders. Neither were there tender caresses or gentle kisses. Only demands and hunger.

Breath heaving, Nathan moved above her. Lightning still flashed sporadically, highlighting her face and hair. Her head was thrown back, her eyes clear and open, when he took her.

Perfect. Naked, damp and dazed, Jackie curled into him while that one word ran around in her head. Nothing had ever been so perfect. His heart was still pounding against hers, his breath still warming her cheek. The rain had slowed, and the thunder was only a murmur in the distance. Storms passed. Some storms.

She hadn't needed the physical act of love to confirm her feelings for Nathan. Lovemaking was only an extension of being in love. But even with her vivid and often far-reaching imagination, she'd never known anything could be like this.

He'd emptied her, and he'd filled her.

No matter how many times they came together, no matter how many years they shared, there would never be another first time. Her eyes closed, her arms wrapped around him, she savored it.

He didn't know what to say to her, or if he was capable of speech at all. He'd thought he knew himself, the man he was and the man he'd chosen to be. The Nathan Powell he'd lived with most of his life wasn't the same man who had plunged so recklessly into passion, giving and taking with greedy disregard.

He'd lost all sense of time, of place, even of self, as he'd driven himself restlessly, even abandonedly, into her. The way he had never done before. The way, he already understood, he would never do again. Unless it was with Jackie.

He should have taken her with more care, and certainly with more consideration. But once begun he had lost whatever foothold he'd still had on reason and had cartwheeled off the cliff with her.

It had been what she'd wanted—what he'd wanted—but did that make it right? There had been no words, no questions. He hadn't even given a thought to his responsibility or her protection. That had made him wince a bit even as he stroked a hand through her hair.

They'd have to talk about that, and soon, because he was going to have to admit that what had happened between them was going to happen again. That didn't make it permanent, he assured himself as his hand fitted possessively over the curve of her shoulder.

"Jack?"

When she tilted her head to look up at him, he was struck by such an unexpected wave of tenderness that he couldn't speak at all. Lips curved, she leaned closer and pressed them to his. It took no more than that to have the embers of desire glowing again. The fingers that had been stroking her hair tightened and dragged her closer. Limber and sleek, she shifted onto him.

"I love you, Nathan. No, don't say anything." Her lips nibbled and rubbed against his as she sought to soothe more than to arouse. "You don't have to say anything. I just need to tell you. And I want to make love with you again and again."

Her hands had already told him as much, and now her mouth was moving lower, nipping and gliding along his neck. His response was so immediate it stunned him.

"Jack, wait a minute."

"No more complaints," she murmured. "I ravished you once, and I can do it again."

"Thank God for that, but wait." Firmly now, thinking only of her, he drew her away by the shoulders. "We have to talk a minute."

"We can talk when we're old—though I did want to mention that I'm crazy about your carpet."

"I've grown fond of it myself. Now, hold on," he said again when she tried to squirm away from his restraining hands. "Jack, I'm serious."

She let out a huge and exaggerated sigh. "Do you have to be?"

"Yes."

"All right, then." She composed her features and settled herself comfortably. "Shoot."

"I'm already doing it backward," he began, furious with himself. "But I don't intend to make the same mistake again. Things happened so quickly before that I never asked, never even thought to ask, if it was all right."

"Of course it was all right," she began with a laugh. "Oh." Her brows rose as realization struck. "You really are a very good man, aren't you?" Despite his grip on her shoulders, she managed to kiss him. "Yes, it's all right. I realize I look like a scatterbrain, but I'm not. Well, at least I'm a responsible one."

The tenderness crept back unexpectedly, and he cupped her face in his hands. "You don't look like a scatterbrain. You may act like one, but you look beautiful."

"Now I know I'm getting to you." She tried to say it lightly, but her eyes glistened. "I'd like you to think I'm beautiful. I always wanted to be."

Her hair fell over her brow, tempting him to brush at it, to tangle his fingers in it. "The first time I saw you, when I was tired and annoyed and you were sitting in my whirlpool, I thought you were beautiful."

"And I thought you were Jake."

"What?"

"I'd been sitting there, thinking about my story, and about Jake—the way he looked, you know." Her fingers roamed over his face as she remembered. "Build, coloring, features. I opened my eyes and saw you and thought... there he is." She rested her cheek on his chest. "My hero."

Troubled, he curled an arm around her. "I'm no hero, Jack."

"You are to me." She shimmied up his body a bit, then rested her forehead against his. "Nathan, I forgot the strudel."

"Did you? What strudel?"

"The apple strudel I made for dessert. Why don't I dish some out and we can eat it in bed?"

Later, he thought, later he'd think about Jackie's idea of love and heroes. "Sounds very sensible."

"Okay." She kissed the tip of his nose, then smiled. "Your bed or mine?"

"Mine," he murmured, as though the word had been waiting to be said. "I want you in mine."

Laziness was its own reward. Jackie embraced the idea as she stretched in bed. Nothing seemed more glorious at the moment than to sleep in after so many

days of rising early and going straight to the typewriter.

She snuggled, half dozing, pretending she was
twelve and it was Saturday. There had been nothing
she'd liked better at twelve than Saturdays. But as she
shifted her leg brushed against Nathan's. It took no
more than that for her to be very, very glad she was no
longer twelve.

"Are you awake?" she asked without opening her
eyes.

"No." His arm came around her possessively and
remained.

Still drowsy, a smile just forming on her lips, she
nibbled on him. "Would you like to be?"

"Depends." He shifted closer to her, enjoying the
quiet, cozy feel of warm body against warm body.
"Did we get all the strudel out of the bed?"

"Can't say for sure. Shall I look?" With that,
Jackie tossed the sheets over their heads and attacked
him.

She had more energy than she was entitled to, Nathan thought later as she lay sprawled over him. The
sheets were now balled and twisted somewhere below
their feet. Still trying to catch his breath, he kept his
eyes half-shut as he looked at her.

She was long and lean and curved very subtly. Her
skin was gold in the late-morning light, except for a
remarkably thin line over her hips where it remained
white, unexposed to the sun. Tousled from the pillow
and from his hands, her hair sprang in a distracted
halo.

He'd always thought he preferred long hair on a
woman, but with Jackie's short, free-swinging style he

could stroke the curve at the back of her neck. He did so now, and she began to purr like a satisfied cat.

What was he going to do with her?

The idea of nudging her gently along was no longer even a remote possibility. He wanted her with him. Needed her. *Need.* That was a word he'd always been careful to avoid. Now that it had slammed into him, he hadn't any idea how to handle it.

He tried to think of what he would do tomorrow, a week, even a month from now, without her. His mind remained stubbornly blank. This wasn't like him. He hadn't been like himself since she'd spun her way into his life.

What did she want from him? Nathan detested himself because he knew he wouldn't ask her. He already knew what she wanted, as if it had been discussed and debated and deliberated. She loved him, at least for today. And he . . . he cared for her. Love was one four-letter word he wouldn't allow himself. Love meant promises. He never made promises unless he was sure he could keep them. A promise given casually and broken was worse than a lie.

With the morning sun shining through the windows and the birds singing the praises of spring, he wished it could be as simple as Jackie would like it. Love, marriage, family. He knew all too well that love didn't guarantee the success of a marriage and that marriage didn't equal family.

His parents had a marriage in which love no longer was an issue. No one would ever have accused the three of them of being a family.

He wasn't his father, Nathan thought as he held Jackie and studied the ceiling. He'd made certain that he would never be his father. But he understood the pride in success and the drive for accomplishment that had been his father's. That were still his father's. And were his.

He shook his head. He hadn't thought of his father or his lack of family life as much in a decade as he had since he'd met Jackie. She did that to him, as well. She made him consider possibilities that he'd rejected long ago with perfect logic and sense. She made him wish and regret what he'd never had reason to wish or regret before.

He couldn't let himself love her, because then he would make promises. And when the promises were broken he'd hate himself. She deserved better than what he could give her or, more accurately, what he couldn't give her.

"Nathan?"

"Hmmm."

"What are you thinking about?"

"You."

When she lifted her head, her eyes were unexpectedly solemn. "I hope not."

Puzzled, he combed his fingers through the tangle of her hair. "Why?"

"Because you're tensing up again." Something came and went in her face—the first shadow of sorrow he'd ever seen in it. "Don't regret. I don't think I could bear it."

"No." He drew her up to cradle her in his arms. "No, I don't. How could I?"

She turned her face into his throat. He didn't know she was forcing back tears, and she couldn't have explained them to him. "I love you, Nathan, and I don't want you to regret that, either, or worry about it. I want you to just let things happen as they're meant to happen.''

He tilted her head back with a finger under her chin. Her eyes were dry now. His were intense. "And that's enough for you?"

"Enough for today." The smile was back. Even he couldn't detect the effort it cost her. "I never know what's going to be enough for tomorrow. How do you feel about brunch? You haven't had my crepes yet. I make really wonderful crepes, but I don't remember if there's any whipping cream. There's always omelets, of course—if the mushrooms haven't dried up. Or we could make do with leftover strudel. Maybe we should have a swim first, and then—"

"Jack?"

"Uh-huh?"

"Shut up."

"Right now?" she asked as his hand slid down to her hip.

"Yes."

"Okay."

She started to laugh, but his lips met hers with such quiet, such fragile tenderness that the laughter became a helpless moan. Her eyes, once alight with amusement, shuttered closed at the sound. She was a strong woman, often valiant in her way, but she had no defense against tenderness.

It had been just as unexpected for him. There had been no flash of fire, no rumble of thunder. Just warmth, a drugging, languorous warmth that crept under his skin, into his brain, into his heart. With one kiss, one easy merging of lips, she filled him.

He hadn't thought of her as delicate. But she was delicate now, as her bones seemed to dissolve under his hands, leaving her smaller somehow, softer. Woman at her most vulnerable. As the kiss spun out, he lifted a hand to her cheek, as if to hold her there, captive.

Patience. She'd known there was a steady, rock-solid patience in him. But until now he'd never shown it to her. Compassion. That, too, she'd sensed in him. But to feel it now, to have him give her the gift of it, was more precious than diamonds. She was lost in him again, not in the frantic race she'd become used to, but in a slow, lengthy search she already knew would lead her where she had always wanted to go.

He caressed where he'd once taken greedily. Her skin was like satin and shivered under his touch. There was a fluidity to her now rather than a frenzy, a quiescence that had taken the place of energy.

His fingertips skimmed over her, and he delighted in making discoveries in territory already conquered. The same woman, yet a different one; her generosity was still there, but merged now with a vulnerability that humbled him. He found her flavor somehow sweeter. When he pressed his lips to her breast, he felt her heartbeat. It hammered fast, not with the heady, energetic rhythm of their past loving, but quick and light.

Experimentally he ran a finger over the inside of her wrist, feeling her pulse beating there, as well. For him. Curling his fingers through hers, he brought them to his lips to kiss and caress them one by one.

The bottom seemed to drop out of her world. With each touch she had fallen deeper, still deeper, into his. Into him. Now, as he did nothing more than brush his mouth over her fingertips, she tumbled headfirst into the dark, trusting him implicitly to catch her.

He could have asked her anything, demanded anything. In that moment her love was so overwhelming that she would have granted any wish without a thought to self or survival. It wasn't possible for her to gather him close and take their loving to another plane. He had a prisoner. Though he might not know it, she would stay enslaved as long as he'd have her.

He only knew that something had changed yet again. He was protector now as well as lover, giver as well as taker. The excitement that knowledge brought was tinged with a trace of fear he struggled to ignore. He couldn't think about tomorrow and tomorrow's consequences when he wanted her, possibly more, impossibly more, than he had only moments ago. She wouldn't object if he took her quickly, if he dragged them both to the top without preamble or delicacy. Perhaps it was because of that, because he understood that she would accept him on any terms, that he found himself needing to give her everything he could.

Slow loving. Almost tortuous. Tender stroking. Lazy tastes. There were quiet sighs that rippled the air until even the sunlight seemed to dim. If it had been possible, he would have had flowers for her, a banquet of them. Soft petals, shimmering fragrances; he would have poured them over her skin. But he only had himself.

It was enough. He was more than enough for her. She showed him that in the way her lips parted, in the way her arms encircled him. No dream she'd ever indulged in, no wish she'd ever given herself, could compare with the reality of him cherishing her.

His hands were so cool, so calm, on her skin. With each touch she felt herself glow. The heat came from within her now, so that it was possible to bank it, to prevent it from becoming overpowering. Just flickers of flame, burning softly.

As gentle as he, she reached for him, offering the pleasure and temptation of unconditional love. When she trembled, he murmured. In reassurance. And she, who had never believed she would need a man to watch over her, understood that she would wither to dust without him.

Generosity, given without restrictions. That she offered, openhanded, was no longer a surprise to him. But to discover that he could give equally, to find that he was compelled to match her, was something new.

He slipped into her, and the tenderness remained.

Slow, harmonious movements. A breath caught, then sighed away like the wind. With his mouth on hers, they continued. Like a Viennese waltz, their dance was light and elegant. When the tempo increased, they surged with the music, spinning, whirling, their eyes open and locked together.

The dance ended as gently as it had begun.

The sun was higher now. Contentedly, her body curved into his, Jackie watched the curtains move with the faint breeze. If she concentrated hard enough she could catch the light fragrance of flowers from the garden below. Nothing identifiable, but a mixture of scents that spoke of spring and new life.

Every moment of the hours they'd had together were lodged firmly in her mind. She knew she would take them out often and enjoy them over and over.

"You know what I'd like?" she asked him.

"Hmmm?" If he hadn't been so dazed, it would have amazed him that he could be dozing in bed this close to noon.

"To stay here, right here in this bed, all day."

"We've got a pretty good start."

Her grin wicked, she turned to face him. Nose to nose, she leered. "Why don't we—" She swore when the phone rang. "It's the wrong number," she told him, climbing over his shoulder as he reached for it. "It's just a woman with a squeaky voice who's going to tell you your name's been selected in a sweepstakes and you've won ten free magazine subscriptions as long as you pay $7.75 a month for handling."

He hesitated a moment because when she said it it was too easy to believe. "What if it isn't?"

"Ah, but what if it is? Do you have enough willpower to resist ten free magazines a month? Be sure, Nathan. Be very sure."

He put a hand over her face and shoved her back against the pillows. "Hello."

"You were warned," Jackie said in a voice that spoke of doom. This time he put the pillow over her face.

"Carla?"

"Carla?" Her voice was muffled by the pillows. Jackie tossed it aside and sank her teeth into his shoulder.

"Ouch! Damn it! No, Carla, I— What is it?" To protect himself, Nathan rolled and trapped Jackie under him. "Yes, I was expecting that." Ignoring the flailing arms and muttered curses beneath him, Nathan listened. "All right, we'll push up the schedule if necessary. No, I've already taken care of that from here. Set this up for tomorrow. Nine. Ten, then," he said. "Contact Cody. I'll want him there. Fine, Carla." Jackie wriggled beneath him and made loud gasping noises. He ignored that, as well. "Yes, I've enjoyed having a few days of relaxation. See you tomorrow."

When he leaned over to hang up the receiver, Jackie managed to squirm out from under him. Face flushed, pulling in exaggerated gulps of air, she thudded a pillow over his head.

"So," she began. "You decided to smother me so that you could run off with the Italian countess and make mad, illicit passion in the Holiday Inn. Don't try to deny it," she warned. "The signs are all too clear."

"Okay. Which Italian countess was that?"

"Carla." She slammed the pillow at him again, aiming lower, then had to bite back a laugh when he grabbed her around the waist. "No, don't try to make up, Nathan. It's too late. I've already decided to murder both you and the countess. I'll electrocute you while you're sharing your bubble bath. No jury would convict me."

"Not if they did a psychiatric profile first."

She made another grab, this time for a very vulnerable area. He avoided her by throwing her onto her back and once again using his body to shield and protect himself. Arms locked, they rolled. Nathan was just beginning to enjoy it when her momentum sent them tumbling to the floor.

Out of breath and rubbing his shoulder, he narrowed his eyes. "You are crazy."

Jackie straddled him and planted her arms on either side of his head. "Okay, Powell, if you value your life, come clean. Who's Carla?"

He considered her. Her eyes were bright, her cheeks flushed with amusement. Her wide, incredible mouth was curved. Casually he cupped her hips in his hands. "You want the truth?"

"And nothing but."

"The countess Carla Mandolini and I have been having a blazing adulterous affair for years. She fools her husband, the elderly and impotent count, by doubling as my secretary. The fool actually believes that the twins are his."

He really was adorable, Jackie decided as she leaned closer. "A likely story," she told him just before her mouth covered his.

Chapter Nine

All right, Nathan, consider yourself kidnapped. You might as well go peacefully."

As he wrapped a towel around his waist, Nathan glanced up. Without bothering to knock, Jackie pushed open the door to the bathroom and strode in. He should be used to it by now, he thought as he secured the towel. She could pop up anytime and anywhere.

"Mind if I put my shoes on?"

"You've got ten minutes."

Before she could turn to go, he had her by the arm. "Where have you been?"

He was becoming too attached to her, Nathan told himself even as the words came out. When he'd woken up alone that morning it had taken all of his control not to dash around the house looking for her. They'd been lovers three days, and already he felt bereft if she wasn't beside him when he opened his eyes in the morning.

"Some of us have work to do, even on Saturdays." She let her gaze roam down, then up. He was damp, tanned and mostly naked. She thought it a pity she'd made plans. "Downstairs in ten minutes, or I'll make you suffer."

"What's going on, Jack?"

"You're not in a position to ask questions." With a last smile, she left him. He heard her run lightly downstairs.

What did she have in store for him now? Nathan wondered as he reached for his razor. With Jackie there were never any guarantees, and there was rarely any rhyme or reason. It should have annoyed him, he thought as he lathered his face. It was supposed to annoy him. He'd already planned his day.

A few hours in his office dealing with the preliminaries on the Sydney project and snipping any loose ends from Denver would take care of the morning. After that he'd thought it might be nice to treat Jackie, and himself, to lunch and tennis at the country club. Being kidnapped hadn't been in his plans.

But he wasn't annoyed. Nathan brought the razor over lather and beard in short, smooth strokes. Because he'd left the window open, the mirror was only lightly steamed at the edges. He could see himself clearly. What had changed?

He was still Nathan Powell, a man with certain responsibilities and priorities. It wasn't a stranger looking back at him in the mirror, but a man he knew very well. The eyes were the same, as was the shape of the face, the hairline. If he looked the same, why didn't he feel the same? More, why couldn't he, a man who knew himself so well, put his finger on exactly what his feelings were?

Shaking the thought aside, he rinsed off the traces of lather. It was absurd. He was exactly who he had always been. The only change in his life was Jackie.

And what the hell was he going to do about her?

It wasn't a question he could avoid much longer. The more involved he became with her, the more certain he was that he was going to hurt her. That was something he would regret the rest of his life. In a matter of weeks he would have to leave her to go to Denver. He couldn't leave her with promises and vows, nor could he expect her to stay when he couldn't tell her what she needed to hear.

He wanted to believe she was nothing more than a few colorful pages in the very straightforward book of his life. But he knew, he already knew, that as his life went on he would keep turning back to look over those few pages again and again.

They should talk. He slapped on after-shave that left his skin cool and stinging. It was up to him to see that they did, quietly, seriously and as soon as possible. The world, as much as he might now wish it could be, was not composed of two people. And neither of them had begun to live the moment they'd met.

"You're running out of time, Nathan."

Jackie's voice came rushing up the stairs and caught him daydreaming. Daydreams were also something new in his life. Swearing at himself, Nathan whipped off the towel and began to dress.

He found her in the kitchen, securing the lid on a cooler, while on the radio some group from the fifties harmonized about love and devotion.

"You're lucky I decided to be generous and give you another five minutes." She turned to study him. He wore black shorts with a white shirt, and his hair was still slightly damp. "I guess it was worth it."

He was almost but not quite used to her frank and unabashed appraisals. "What's going on, Jack?"

"I told you. You're kidnapped." She stepped forward to slip her arms around his waist. "If you try to escape, it'll go hard on you." Pressing her face in his throat, she began to sniff. "I love your after-shave."

"What's in the cooler?"

"Surprises. Sit down, you can have some cereal."

"Cereal?"

"Man doesn't live by hotcakes alone, Nathan." She kissed him quick. "And some bananas." She moved away to get one, changed her mind and took two. As she peeled her own, she began to explain. "You might as well consider yourself my hostage for the day and make this simple."

"Make what simple?"

"We've both been working hard the last few days— well, except for one very memorable day." She smiled as she took the first bite. "And that was exhausting in its own way. So..." She slapped a palm on the cooler. "I'm taking you for a ride."

"I see." Nathan sliced the banana over a bowl of cornflakes. "Anywhere in particular?"

"No. Anywhere at all. You eat, I'll put this in the boat."

"Boat?" He paused, the banana peel in his hand. "My boat?"

"Of course." Hefting the cooler, she turned back with an easy smile. "As much as I love you, Nathan, I know even you can't walk on water. Coffee's hot, by the way, but make it quick, will you?"

He did, because he was more interested in what she had up her sleeve than in a bowl of cold cereal. She'd left the radio on, he supposed for his benefit. After he'd rinsed his bowl, Nathan switched it off. As a matter of course he went to check the front door. Jackie had left it open. He shut it, locked it, then went to join her.

Outside, he found her competently storing supplies in the hatch. She wore a visor in a blazing orange that matched her shorts and the frames of a pair of mirrored wraparound sunglasses.

"All set?" she asked him. "Cast off, will you?"

"You're driving?"

"Sure. I was practically born on a boat." She slipped behind the wheel and tossed a look over her shoulder as Nathan hesitated, his hands on the line. "Trust me. I looked at a map."

"Well, then." Wondering if he was taking his life in his hands, he cast off and came aboard.

"Sun block," she said, handing him a tube. With that she pulled smoothly away from the dock. "How do you feel about St. Thomas?"

"Jack..."

"Only kidding. I've thought what a kick it would be to travel the whole Intracoastal. Take a whole summer and just cruise."

He'd thought of it, too, as something he might find time for—someday. After retirement, perhaps. When Jackie said it, it seemed possible it could happen tomorrow. And it made him wish it would happen tomorrow. He only murmured as he watched her handle the boat.

He should have known she'd be fine. Maybe she couldn't remember to close doors behind her, but it seemed to him that whatever she did she did with careless skill. Her hand was light on the wheel as she negotiated the channel. Even when she picked up speed, he relaxed.

"You picked a good day for a kidnapping."

"I thought so." She threw him a grin, then settled more comfortably in her seat.

The boat handled like a dream. Of course, she'd known that Nathan would keep it in tip-top shape. That was one of the things she admired about him. He didn't take his possessions for granted. If it belonged to him, it deserved his attention. Too many people she knew, herself included, could develop a casual disregard for what was theirs. She'd learned something from him about pride of possession and the responsibility that went along with it.

She belonged to him now. Jackie hoped he'd begin to care for her with the same kind of devotion.

You're moving too fast, as usual, she cautioned herself. Caution was something else she'd learned from Nathan. It had to be enough, for now, that he no longer looked alarmed whenever she told him she loved him. The fact that he was beginning to accept that she did was a giant step. And soon—eventually, she thought, correcting herself—eventually he would accept the fact that he loved her back.

She knew he did. It wasn't a matter of wish fulfillment or hopeful dreams. She saw it when he looked at her, felt it when he touched her. Because she did, it made it that much more difficult to wait.

She'd always looked for instant gratification. Even as a child she'd been able to learn quickly and apply what she'd learned so that the rewards came quickly. Writing had shown her more than a love for storytelling. It had also shown her that some rewards were best waited for. Having Nathan, really having him, would be worth waiting a lifetime.

She turned down an alley of water where the bush was thick and green. It was hardly wide enough for two boats to pass. Near the verges, limbs of deadwood poked through the surface like twisted arms. Behind them the wake churned white, while ahead the water was darker, more mysterious. Above, the sun was a white flash, hinting, perhaps threatening, of the sultry summer still weeks away. Spray flew, glinting in the light. The motor purred, sending a flurry of birds rocketing above the trees.

"Ever been on the Amazon?"

"No." Nathan turned to her. "Have you?"

"Not yet," she told him, as if it were only a small oversight. "It might be something like this. Brown water, thick vegetation hiding all sorts of dangerous jungle life. Is it crocodiles or alligators down there?"

"I couldn't say."

"I'll have to look it up." A dragonfly dashed blue and gleaming across the bow, catching her attention. It skimmed over the water without making a ripple,

then flashed into the bush. "It's wonderful here."
Abruptly she cut the engine.

"What are you doing?"

"Listening."

Within moments the birds began to call, rustling
through the leaves and growing bold in the silence.
Insects sent up a soprano chorus. There was a watery
plop, then two, as a frog swallowed an insect for an
early lunch. Even the water itself had sound, a low,
murmurous voice that invited laziness. From far off,
too far off to be important, came the hum of another
boat.

"I used to love to go camping," Jackie remembered. "I'd drag one of my brothers, and—"

"I didn't know you had any brothers."

"Two. Fortunately for me, they've both taken an
avid interest in my father's many empires, leaving me
free to do as I please." He couldn't see her eyes as she
spoke, but from the tone of her voice he knew they
were smiling.

"Never any interest in being a corporate climber?"

"Oh, God, no. Well, actually, I did think of being
chairman of the board when I was six. Then I decided
I'd rather be a brain surgeon. So I was more than
happy when Ryan and Brandon took me off the
hook." Lazily she slipped out of her deck shoes to
stretch her toes. "I've always thought it would be difficult to be a son of a demanding father and not want
to follow in his footsteps."

She'd said it casually, but Nathan was so completely silent that she realized she'd hit part of the
mark. She opened her mouth to question, then shut it
again. In his own time, she reminded herself. "Any-

way, even though it often took blackmail to get one of my brothers to go with me, I really loved sitting by the fire and listening. You could be anywhere you wanted to be.''

''Where did you go?''

''Oh, here and there. Arizona was the best. There's something indescribable about the desert when you're sitting beside a tent.'' She grinned again. ''Of course, there's also something special about the presidential suite and room service. Depends on the mood. You want to drive?''

''No, you're doing fine.''

With a laugh, Jackie kicked the motor on. ''I hate to say it, but you ain't seen nothin' yet.''

She spun the boat through the waterway, taking any out-of-the-way canal or inlet that caught her fancy. She was delighted to chug along behind the *Jungle Queen*, Lauderdale's triple-decker party boat, and wave to the tourists. For a time she was content to follow its wake and direction as it toured the Intracoastal's estates.

The houses pleased her, with their sweeping grounds and sturdy pillars. She enjoyed the flood of the spring flowers and the wink and shimmer of the pools. When another boat passed, she'd make up stories about the occupants that had Nathan laughing or just rolling his eyes.

It pleased her just as much to turn off the more traveled routes and pretend she was lost in the quiet, serpentine waters where the brush grew heavy and close at the edges. Shutting down again under the shade of bending palms and cypress, she took out Jackie's idea of a picnic.

There was Pouilly-Fuissé in paper cups, and cracked crab to be dug out with plastic forks, and tiny Swiss meringues, white and glossy. After she'd badgered Nathan into taking off his shirt, she rubbed sun block over him, rambling all the while about the idea of setting a book in the Everglades.

But what she noticed most as she stroked the cream over his skin was that he was relaxed. There was no band of tension over his shoulders, no knot of nerves at the base of his neck. When he reciprocated by applying the cream to wherever her skinny blue tank top exposed her skin, there was none in her, either.

When the cooler was packed away again, she jumped back behind the wheel. The morning laziness was over, she told him. Turning the boat around, she headed out.

She burst into Port Everglades to join the pleasure and cruise ships, the freighters and sailboats. Here the water was wide and open, the spray cool and the air full of sound.

"Do you ever come here?" she shouted.

"No." Nathan clamped a hand on the orange visor she'd transferred from her head to his. "Not often."

"I love it! Think of all the places these ships have been before they come here. And where they're going when they leave. Hundreds of people, thousands, come here on their way to—I don't know . . . Mexico, Cuba."

"The Amazon?"

"Yes." Laughing, she turned the boat in a circle that had spray spurting up the sides. "There are so many places to go and see. You don't live long enough, you just can't live long enough to do everything you should.'' Her hair danced madly away from her face as she rode into the wind. ''That's why I'm coming back.''

''To Florida?''

''No. To life.''

He watched her laugh again and raise her arm to another boat. If anyone could, Nathan thought, it would be Jackie.

He let her have her head. Indeed, he didn't know if he could have stopped her if he'd been inclined to. Besides, he'd long since acknowledged that he enjoyed the race.

At midafternoon, she pulled up to a dock and advised Nathan to secure the lines. While he obliged, she dug her purse out of the hatch.

''Where are we going now?''

''Shopping.''

He held out a hand to help her onto the pier. ''For what?''

''For anything. Maybe nothing.'' With her hand in his, she began to walk. ''You know, spring break's nearly here. In a couple of weeks the college crowd will flock to this, the mecca of the East.''

''Don't remind me.''

''Oh, don't be a stick-in-the-mud, Nathan. Kids have to blow off steam, too. But I was thinking the shops would be a madhouse then, and as much as I might appreciate that, you wouldn't, so we should do this now.''

''Do what now?''

''Shop,'' she explained patiently. ''Play tourist, buy tacky souvenirs and T-shirts with vulgar sayings, haggle over a shell ashtray.''

"I can't tell you how much I appreciate you thinking of me."

"My pleasure, darling." She planted a quick kiss on his cheek. "Listen, unless I miss my guess, this is something you never do."

He was surprised when she paused, waiting for his answer. "No, it's not."

"It's time you did." She adjusted the visor to a cockier angle. "You very sensibly moved south and chose Fort Lauderdale because of its growth, but you don't take too many walks on the beach."

"I thought we were going shopping."

"It's the same thing." She slipped her arm around his waist. "You know, Nathan, as far as I can see, you don't have one T-shirt with a beer slogan, a rock concert or an obscene saying."

"I've been deprived."

"I know. That's why I'd like to help you out."

"Jack." He stopped, turning around to gently take her shoulders. "Please don't."

"You'll thank me later."

"We'll compromise. I'll buy a tie."

"Only if it has a naked mermaid on it."

Jackie found exactly what she wanted bordering Las Olas Boulevard. There was a labyrinth of small cross streets bulging with shops selling everything from snorkels to sapphires. Telling him it was for his own good, Jackie dragged him into a small, crowded store with a doorway flanked by two garish red flamingos.

"They're becoming entirely too trendy," she said to Nathan with a flick of her hand toward the slim-legged birds. "It's a shame I'm so fond of them. Oh, look, just what I've always wanted. A music box with shells stuck all over it. What do you suppose it plays?''

Jackie wound up what Nathan considered one of the most hideous-looking things he'd ever seen. It played "Moon River."

"No." Jackie shook her head over the melody. "I can do without that."

"Thank God."

Chuckling, she replaced it and began to poke through rows of equally moronic whatnots. "I understand, Nathan, that you have an eye for the aesthetic and harmonious, but there really is something to be said for the ugly and useless."

"Yes, but I can't say it here. There are children present."

"Now take this."

"No," he said as she held up a pelican made entirely of clamshells. "Please, I can't thank you enough for the thought, but I couldn't."

"Only for demonstration purposes. This has a certain charm." She laughed as his brow rose. "No, really. Think of this. Say a couple comes here on their honeymoon and they want something silly and very personal to remember the day by. They need something they can look at in ten years and bring back that very heady, very intimate time before insurance payments and wet diapers." She flourished the bird. *"Voilà."*

"Voilà? One doesn't *voilà* a pelican, especially a shell one."

"More imagination," she said with a sigh. "All you need is a little more imagination." With what seemed like genuine regret, she set the pelican down. Just when he thought it was safe, Jackie dragged him over to a maze of T-shirts. She seemed very taken with one in teal with an alligator lounging in a hammock drinking a wine cooler. Passing it by, she dragged out one of a grinning shark in dark glasses.

"This," she told him grandly, "is you."

"It is?"

"Absolutely. Not to say you're a predator, but sharks are notorious for being loners, and the sunglasses are a symbol of a need for privacy."

He studied it, frowning and intrigued. "You know, I've never known anyone to be philosophical about T-shirts."

"Clothes make the man, Nathan." Draping it over her arm, she continued to browse. When she loitered by a rack of ties screen-printed with fish, he put his foot down.

"No, Jack, not even for you."

Sighing at his lack of vision, she settled for the shirt.

She hauled him through a dozen shops until pictures of neon palms, plastic mugs and garish straw hats blurred in his head. She bought with a blatant disregard for style or use. Then, suddenly inspired, she shipped off a huge papier-mâché parrot to her father.

"My mother will make him take it off to one of his offices, but he'll love it. Daddy has a wonderful sense of the ridiculous."

"Is that where you get it?"

"I suppose." Hands on her hips, she turned in a circle to be certain she hadn't missed anything. "Well, since I've done that, I'd better run by that little jewelry store and see if there's anything appropriate for my mother." She pocketed the receipt, then relieved Nathan of two packages. "How are you holding up?"

"I'm game if you are."

"You're sweet." She leaned over, between packages, to kiss him. "Why don't I buy you an ice-cream cone?"

"Why don't you?"

She grinned at that, thinking he was certainly coming along. "Right after I find something tasteful for my mother," she promised, and she proved as good as her word.

Some fifteen minutes later, she chose an ebony pin crusted with pearls. It was a very mature, very elegant piece in faultless taste.

The purchase showed Nathan two things. First that she glanced only casually at the price, so casually that he was certain she would have bought it no matter what the amount. An impulse buyer she certainly was, but he sensed that once she'd decided an item was right, the dollar amount was unimportant. And second that the pin was both conventional and elegant, making it a far cry from the parrot she'd chosen for her father.

It made him wonder, as she loitered over some of the more colorful pieces in the shop, if her parents were as different as her vision of them.

He'd always believed, perhaps too strongly, that children inherited traits, good and bad. Yet here was Jackie, nothing like a woman who would wear a classically tasteful pin, and also nothing like a man who had spent his adult life wheeling and dealing in the business world.

Moments later, he had other things to worry about. They were out on the street again, and Jackie was making arrangements to rent a bicycle built for two.

"Jack, I don't think this is—"

"Why don't you put those packages in the basket, Nathan?" She patted his hand before paying for the rental.

"Listen, I haven't been on a bike since I was a teenager."

"It'll come back to you." The transaction complete, she turned to him and smiled. "I'll take the front if you're worried."

Perhaps she hadn't meant to bait him, but he didn't believe it. Nathan swung his leg over and settled on the front seat. "Get on," he told her. "And remember, you asked for it."

"I love a masterful man," she cooed. Nathan found his lips twitching at the phony Southern accent as he set off.

She'd been right. It did come back to him. They pedaled smoothly, even sedately, across the street to ride along the seawall.

Jackie was glad he'd taken the lead. It gave her the opportunity to daydream and sightsee. Which, she thought with a smile, she would have done even if she'd been steering. This way, she didn't have to worry about running into a parked car or barreling down on pedestrians. Nathan could be trusted to steer true. It was only one more reason she loved him.

Matching her rhythm to his, she watched his shoulders. Strong and dependable. She found those both such lovely words. Strange ... she'd never known she would find dependability so fiercely attractive until she'd found it. Found him.

Now he was relaxed, enjoying the sun and the day in it. She could give that to him. Not every day of the week, Jackie mused. He wouldn't always fall in with whatever last-minute plans she cooked up. But often enough, she thought, and wished there wasn't so much space between them so that she could wrap her arms around him and just hug.

He'd never pictured himself biking along the oceanfront—much less enjoying it. The fact was, Nathan rarely even came to this section of town. It was for tourists and teenagers. Being with Jackie made him feel like both. She was showing him new things not only about the city where he'd lived for nearly a decade but about the life he'd had more than thirty years to experience.

Everything about her was unexpected. How could he have known that the unexpected could also be the fresh? For a few hours he hadn't given a thought to Denver or penalty clauses or the responsibilities of tomorrow. He hadn't thought of tomorrow at all.

This was today, and the sun was bright, and the water was a rich blue against the golden sand. There were children squealing as they played in the surf, and there was the smell of oils and lotions. Someone was walking a dog along the beach, and a vendor was hawking nachos.

Across the street, beach towels waved colorfully over rails, making a tawdry little hotel seem exotic. He could smell hot dogs, he realized, and some kind of colored ice was being sold to children so that it would drip sticky down their arms as they slurped it. Oddly enough, he had a sudden yen for it himself.

When he looked up, he spotted the black-and-yellow colors of a kite shaped like a wasp. It had caught the wind and was climbing. A light plane flew over, trailing a flowing message about the special at a local restaurant.

He took it all in, wondering why he'd thought the beach held no magic for him. Perhaps it hadn't when he'd been alone.

On impulse, he signaled Jackie, then stopped.

"You owe me some ice cream."

"So I do." She slipped lithely off the bike, kissed him, then backtracked a few steps to a vendor. She considered, debated and studied her choices, taking a longer and more serious deliberation over ice cream on a stick than she had over a five-hundred-dollar brooch. After weighing the pros and cons, she settled on chocolate and nuts wrapped around a slab of vanilla.

Stuffing her change in her pocket, she turned and saw Nathan. He was holding a big orange balloon. "Goes with your outfit," he told her, then gently looped the string around her wrist.

She was going to cry. Jackie felt the tears well up. It was only a ball of colorful rubber held by a string, she knew. But as symbols went, it was the best. She knew that when the air had finally escaped she would press the remains between the pages of a book as sentimentally as she would a rose.

"Thanks," she managed, then dutifully handed him the ice cream before she threw her arms around him.

He held her close, trying not to show the awkwardness he was suddenly feeling. How did a man deal with a woman who cried over a balloon? He'd expected her to laugh. Kissing her temple, he reminded himself that she rarely did the expected.

"You're welcome."

"I love you, Nathan."

"I think maybe you do," he murmured. The idea left him both exhilarated and shaken. What was he going to do about her? He wondered as his arms tightened around her. What the hell was he going to do about her, and them?

Looking up, Jackie saw the concern and the doubt in his eyes. She bit back a sigh, touching his face instead. There was time, she told herself. There was still plenty of time.

"Ice cream's melting." She was smiling as she brushed his lips with hers. "Why don't we sit on the wall while we eat it? Then you can change into your new shirt."

He cupped her chin in his hand, lingering over another kiss. He didn't know Justine had used the word *besotted* in describing his feelings for Jackie, but that was precisely what he was.

"I'm not changing shirts on the street."

She smiled again and took his hand.

When their hour was up, they pedaled back. Nathan was wearing his shark.

Chapter Ten

From the doorway, Jackie watched Nathan drive off. She lifted her hand as his car headed down the street. For a moment there was only the sound of his fading engine breaking the morning quiet. Then, standing there, she heard the neighborhood noises of children being loaded into cars for school, doors slamming, goodbyes and last-minute instructions being given.

Nice sounds, Jackie thought as she leaned against the doorjamb. Regular everyday sounds that would be repeated morning after morning. There was a solidity to them, and a comfort.

She wondered if wives felt this way, seeing off their husbands after sharing that last cup of coffee and before the workday really began. It was an odd mixture of emotions, the pleasure of watching her man tidily on his way and the regret of knowing it would be hours before he came back.

But she wasn't a wife, Jackie reminded herself as she wandered away from the door without remembering to shut it. It didn't do any good to imagine herself as one. It did less good to regret knowing that Nathan was still far from ready for commitments and wedding rings.

It shouldn't be so important.

Chewing on her bottom lip, she started back upstairs. Mrs. Grange was already scrubbing and mopping the kitchen, and she herself had enough work to do to keep her occupied throughout the day. When Nathan came home, he would be glad to see her, and they'd share the casual talk of couples.

It couldn't be so important.

She was happy, after all, happier with Nathan than she'd ever been before or than she could imagine herself being without him. Since there had never been any major tragedies in her life, that was saying quite a lot. He cared for her, and if there were still restrictions on how much he would allow himself to care, what they had now was more than many people ever had.

He laughed more. It was very gratifying to know she'd given him that. Now, when she put her arms around him, it was a rare thing for her to find him tense. She wondered if he knew he reached for her in his sleep and held her close. She didn't think so. His subconscious had already accepted that they belonged together. That they were together. It would take a bit longer for him to accept that consciously.

So she'd be patient. Until Nathan, Jackie hadn't realized she had such an enormous capacity for patience. It pleased her to be able to find a virtue in herself that, because it had so seldom been tapped, seemed to run free.

He'd changed her. Jackie took her seat in front of her typewriter, thinking Nathan probably didn't realize that, either. She hadn't fully realized it herself until it had already happened. She thought of the future more, without the need for rose-colored glasses. She'd come to appreciate the ability to make plans—not that she wouldn't always enjoy an interesting detour, but she'd come to understand that happiness and good times didn't always hinge on impulse.

She'd begun to look at life a little differently. It had come home to her that a sense of responsibility wasn't necessarily a burden. It could also bring a sense of satisfaction and accomplishment. Seeing something through, even when the pace began to drag and the enthusiasm began to wane, was part of living. Nathan had shown her that.

She wasn't certain she could explain it to him so that he would understand or even believe her. After all, she'd never given anyone reason to believe she could be sensible, dependable and tenacious. Things were different now.

Surprised at her own nerves, she looked down at the padded envelope sitting beside the neatly typed pile of manuscript pages. For the first time in her life, she was ready to put herself on the line. To prove herself, Jackie thought, taking a deep breath. To prove herself to herself first, then to Nathan, then to her family.

There was no guarantee that the agent would accept the proposal, nor, though he'd been gracious and marginally encouraging, that he would find anything appealing in her work. Risks didn't frighten her, Jackie told herself. But still she hesitated, not quite able to take the next step and slip the pages into the envelope.

This risk frightened her. It hurt to admit it, but she was scared to death. It was no longer just a matter of telling an entertaining story from start to finish. It was her future on the line now, the future she had once blithely believed could take care of itself. If she failed now, she had no one to blame but herself.

She couldn't, as she had with so many of her other projects, claim that she'd discovered something that interested her more. Writing was it, win or lose, and somehow, though she knew it was foolish, the success or failure of her work was inevitably tied up with her success or failure with Nathan.

She crossed her fingers tight, eyes closed, and recited the first prayer that came into her head, though "Now I lay me down to sleep" wasn't quite appropriate. This done, Jackie shoved the proposal into the bag. Clutching it to her chest, she ran downstairs.

"Mrs. Grange, I've got to go out for a few minutes. I won't be long."

The housekeeper barely glanced up from her polishing. "Take your time."

It was done within fifteen minutes. Jackie stood in front of the post office, certain she'd just made the biggest mistake of her life. She should have gone over the first chapter again. A dozen glaring errors leaped into her mind, errors that seemed so obvious now that the manuscript was sealed and stamped and handed over to some post office clerk she didn't even know.

It occurred to her that there had been a wonderful angle she hadn't bothered to explore and that her characterization of the sheriff was much too weak. He should have chewed tobacco. That was the answer, the perfect answer. All she had to do was go in and stick a wad of tobacco in his mouth and the book would be a best-seller.

She took a step toward the door, stopped and took a step back. She was being ridiculous. Worse, if she didn't get ahold of herself, she was going to be sick. Weak-kneed, she sat on the curb and dropped her head into her hands. Sink or swim, the proposal was going to New York, and it was going today. It amazed her to remember that she'd once thought of celebrating with champagne when she had enough to ship off. She didn't feel like celebrating. She felt like crawling home and burying herself under the covers.

What if she was wrong? Why hadn't she ever considered the fact that she could be totally and completely wrong—about the book, about Nathan, about herself? Only a fool, only a stupid fool, left herself without any route to survival.

She'd poured her heart into that story, then sent it off to a relative stranger who would then have the authority to give a thumbs-up or a thumbs-down without any regard for her as a person. It was business.

She'd given her heart to Nathan. She'd held it out to him in both hands and all but forced him to take it. If he tried to give it back to her, no matter how gently he handled it, it would be cracked and bruised.

There were tears on her cheeks. Feeling them, Jackie let out a little huff of disgust and dragged the heels of her hands over them. What a pitiful sight. A grown woman sitting on a curb crying because things might not work out the way she wanted them to. She sniffled, then rose to her feet. Maybe they wouldn't work out and she'd have to deal with it. But in the meantime she was going to do her damnedest to win.

By noon, Jackie was sitting at the counter, elbows up, looking at Mrs. Grange's latest pictures of her grandchildren while they shared a pasta salad.

"These are great. This one here...Lawrence, right?"

"That's Lawrence. He's three. A pistol."

Jackie studied the little towhead with the smear of what might have been peanut butter on his chin. "Looks like a heartbreaker to me. Do you get to spend much time with them?"

"Oh, now and again. Don't seem enough, though, with grandkids. They grow up faster than your own. This one, Anne Marie, she favors me." A big knuckled finger tapped a snapshot of a little girl in a frilly blue dress. "Hard to believe now—" Mrs. Grange patted an ample hip "—but I was a good-looking woman a few years and a few pounds back."

"You're still a good-looking woman, Mrs. Grange." Jackie poured out more of the fruit drink she'd concocted. "And you have a beautiful family."

Because the compliment had been given easily, Mrs. Grange accepted it. "Families, they make up for a lot. I was eighteen when I ran off to marry Clint. Oh, he was something to look at, let me tell you. Lean as a snake and twice as mean." She chuckled, the way a woman could over an old and almost faded mistake. "I was what you might call swept away."

She took a bite of pasta as she looked back. It didn't occur to her that she was talking about private things to someone she hardly knew. Jackie made it easy to talk. "Girls got no sense at that age, and I wasn't any different. Marry in haste, they say, but who listens?"

"People who say that probably haven't been lucky enough to have been swept away."

Admiring Jackie's logic, Mrs. Grange smiled. "That's true enough, and I can't say I regret it, even though at twenty-four I found myself in a crowded little apartment without a husband, without a penny, and with four little boys wanting their supper. Clinton had walked out on the lot of us, smooth as you please."

"I'm sorry. It must have been awful for you."

"I've had better moments." She turned then, seeing Jackie looking at her not with polite interest but with eyes filled with sympathy and understanding. "Sometimes we get what we ask for, Miss Jack, and I'd asked for Clint Grange, worthless snake that he was."

"What did you do after he'd left?"

"I cried. Spent the night and the better part of a day at it. It felt mighty good, that self-pity, but my boys needed a mother, not some wet-eyed female pining after her man. So I took a look around, figured I'd made enough of a mess of things for a while and decided to fix what I could. That's when I started cleaning houses. Twenty-eight years later, I'm still cleaning them." She looked around the tidy kitchen with a sense of simple satisfaction. "My kids are grown up, and two of them have families of their own. I guess you might say Clint did me a favor, but I don't think

I'd thank him if we happened to run into each other in the checkout line at the supermarket."

Jackie understood the last of the sentiment, but not the beginning. If a man had left her high and dry with three children, hanging was too good for him. "How do you figure he did you a favor?"

"If he'd stayed with me, I'd never have been the same kind of mother, the same kind of person. I guess you could say that some people change your life by coming into it, and others change it by going out." Mrs. Grange smiled as she finished off her salad. "Course, I don't suppose I'd shed any tears if I heard old Clinton was lying in a gutter somewheres begging for loose change."

Jackie laughed and toasted her. "I like you, Mrs. Grange."

"I like you, too, Miss Jack. And I hope you find what you're looking for with Mr. Powell." She rose then, but hesitated. She'd always been a good mother, but had never been lavish with praise. "You're one of those people who change lives by coming in. You've done something nice for Mr. Powell."

"I hope so. I love him a lot." With a sigh, she stacked Mrs. Grange's snapshots. "That's not always enough, is it?"

"It's better than a stick in the eye." In her gruff way, she patted Jackie's shoulder, then went about her business.

Jackie thought that over, nodded, then walked upstairs, where she went to work with a vengeance.

Long after Mrs. Grange had gone home and afternoon had turned to evening, Nathan found her there.

She was hunched over the machine, posture forgotten, her hair falling into her face and her bare feet hooked around the legs of the chair.

He watched her, more than a little intrigued. He'd never really seen her work before. Whenever he'd come up, she'd somehow sensed his approach and swung around in her chair the moment he'd entered.

Now her fingers would drum on the keys, then stop, drum again, then pause while she stared out of the window as if she'd gone into a trance. She'd begin to type again, frowning at the paper in front of her, then smiling, then muttering to herself.

He glanced over at the pile of pages to her right, unaware that the bulk of them were copies of what she'd mailed that morning. He had an uncomfortable feeling that she was more done than undone by this time. Then he cursed himself for being so selfish. What she was doing was important. He'd understood that since the night she'd spun part of the tale for him. It was wrong of him to wish it wouldn't move so quickly or so well, but he'd come to equate the end of her book with the end of their relationship. Yet he knew, even as he stood in the doorway and watched her, that it was he who would end it, and soon.

It had been a month. Only a month, he thought, dragging a hand through his hair. How had she managed to turn his life upside down in a matter of weeks? Despite all his resolutions, all his plans to the contrary, he'd fallen in love with her. That only made it worse. Loving, he wanted to give her all those pretty, unrealistic promises. Marriage, family, a lifetime. Years of shared days and nights. But all he could give her was disappointment.

It was best, really for the best, that Denver was only two weeks away. Even now the wheels were turning that would keep him at the office and in meetings more and at home less. In twelve days he would get on a plane and head west, away from her. Nathan had come to understand that if he didn't love her, if it were only need now, he might be tempted to make those promises to keep her there.

She deserved better. Despite both of them, he was going to make sure she didn't settle for less.

But there were twelve days left.

Quietly he moved toward her. When her fingers stilled again, he laid his hands on her shoulders. Jackie came off the chair with a yelp.

"I'm sorry," he said, but he had to laugh. "I didn't mean to startle you."

"You didn't. You scared me out of my skin." She sank back into the chair with a hand to her heart. "What are you doing home so early?"

"I'm not. It's after six."

"Oh. No wonder my back feels like it belongs to an eighty-year-old weight lifter."

He began to massage her shoulders. That, too, was something he'd learned from her. "How long have you been at it?"

"I don't know. Lost track. Right there... Mmmm." Sighing her approval, she shifted under his hands. "I was going to set an alarm or something after Mrs. Grange left, but Burt Donley rode into town, and I forgot."

"Burt Donley?"

"The cold-blooded hired hand of Samuel Carlson."

"Oh, of course, Burt."

Chuckling, she looked over her shoulder. "Burt murdered Sarah's father, at Carlson's bidding. He and Jake have unfinished business from Laramie. That's when Burt gunned down Jake's best friend—in the back, of course."

"Of course."

"And how was your day?"

"Not as exciting. No major shootouts or encounters with loose women."

"Lucky for you I happen to be feeling very loose." She rose, sliding her body up his until her arms were linked around his neck. "Why don't I go see what I can mix together for dinner? Then we'll talk about it."

"Jack, you don't have to cook for me every night."

"We made a deal."

He stilled her mouth with a kiss, a longer and more intense one than he'd realized he needed. When he drew away, her eyes had that soft, unfocused look he'd come to love. "I'd say all those bets were off. Wouldn't you?"

"I don't mind cooking for you, Nathan."

"I know." She could have no idea how such a simple statement humbled him. "But I'd guess of the two of us you've had the tougher day." He drew her closer, wanting to smell her hair, brush his lips over her temple. He was hardly aware that his hands had slipped under her shirt just to stroke the long line of her back. "I'd offer to go down and throw something together, but I doubt you'd be able to eat it. Over the past few weeks I've learned my cooking's not just bad, it's embarrassing."

"We could send out for pizza."

"An excellent idea." He drew her toward the bed. "In an hour."

"An even better idea," she murmured, and melted into him.

Later, much later, after the sun had set and the cicadas had started their serenade, they sat on the patio, an empty carton between them and wine growing warm in glasses. The silence between them had stretched out, long and comfortable. Lovemaking and food had left them content. There was an ease between that usually came only from years of friendship or from complete understanding.

The moon was round and white and generous with its light. With her legs stretched out and her eyes half closed, Jackie decided she could happily stay where she was for hours. It could be like this, just like this, she thought, for the rest of her life.

"You know, Nathan, I've been thinking."

"Hmm?" He stirred himself enough to look at her. Moonlight did something special to her skin, to her eyes. Though he knew he would remember her best in the sunlight, with energy vibrating through her, there would be times when he would need a memory like this—of Jackie, almost bonelessly relaxed, in the light of a full moon.

"Are you listening?"

"No, I'm looking. There are times you are incredibly lovely."

She smiled, almost shyly, then reached out to take his hands. "Keep that up and I won't be able to think at all."

"Is that all it takes?"

"Do you want to hear my idea or not?"

"I'm never sure if I want to hear your ideas."

"This is a good one. I think we should have a party."

"A party?"

"Yes, you know what a party is, Nathan. A social gathering, often including music, food, drink and a group of people brought together for entertainment purposes."

"I've heard of them."

"Then we've passed the first hurdle." She kissed his hand, but he could tell that her mind was already leaping forward. "You've been back from Europe for weeks now and you haven't seen any of your friends. You do have friends, don't you?"

"One or two."

"There we go, over the second hurdle." Lazily she stretched out her legs, rubbing the arch of her foot over his calf. "As a businessman and a pillar of the community—I'm sure you're a pillar of the community—it's practically your obligation to entertain."

He lifted a brow. "I've never been much of a pillar, Jack."

"That's where you're wrong. Anyone who wears a suit the way you do is an absolute pillar." She grinned at him, knowing she'd ruffled his feathers. "A man of distinction, that's you, darling. A tower of strength and conservatism. A dyed-in-the-wool Republican."

"How do you know I'm a Republican?"

Her smile became sympathetic. "Please, Nathan, let's not debate the obvious. Have you ever owned a foreign car?"

"I don't see what that has to do with it."

"Never mind, your politics are entirely your affair." She patted his hand. "Myself, I'm a political agnostic. I'm not entirely convinced they exist. But we're getting off the subject."

"What else is new?"

"Let's talk party, Nathan." As she spoke, she leaned closer, enthusiasm already bubbling. "You've got those fat little address books at every phone in the house. I'm sure out of them you could find enough convivial bodies to make up a party."

"Convivial bodies?"

"A party's nothing without them. It doesn't have to be elaborate—just a couple dozen people, some nice little canapés and an air of good cheer. It could be a combination welcome-home and bon-voyage party for you."

He glanced over sharply at that. Her eyes were steady and a great deal more serious than her words. So, she was thinking about Denver, too. It was like her not to have mentioned it directly or to have asked questions. His fingers tightened on hers. "When did you have in mind?"

She could smile again. Now that his leaving had been brought up and acknowledged, she could push it firmly to the back of her mind. "How about next week?"

"All right. I have an agency we can call."

"No, a party's personal."

"And a lot of work."

She shook her head. She wasn't able to explain that she needed something to keep her mind occupied. "Don't worry, Nathan. If there's one thing I know how to do, it's throw a party. You take care of contacting your friends. I'll do the rest."

"If that's what you want."

"Very much. Now that that's settled, how about a swim?"

He glanced over at the pool. It was inviting and tempting, but so was sitting doing nothing. "Go ahead. The idea of changing into a suit seems too complicated."

"Who needs a suit?" To prove a point, she rose and shimmied out of her shorts.

"Jack . . ."

"Nathan," she said, mimicking his tone, "one of the ten great pleasures of life is skinny-dipping in the moonlight." The thin bikinis she wore joined her shorts. Her baggy T-shirt skimmed her thighs. "You have a very private pool here," she continued. "Your neighbors would need a stepladder and binoculars to sneak a peak." Carelessly she pulled the T-shirt over her head and stood, slim and naked. "If they want to that badly, we may as well oblige them."

His mouth went dry. He should have been beyond that by now. Over the past few weeks he'd seen, touched, tasted every inch of her. Yet watching Jackie poised at the edge of the pool, her body gold and gleaming in the moonlight, made his heart thud like a teenager's on a first date.

She rose on her toes, arched and dived cleanly into the water. And surfaced, laughing. "God, I've missed this." Her body glimmered beneath the surface, darker and somehow more lush with the illusion of moonlight and water. "I used to sneak out at one in the morning to swim like this. My mother would have been horrified, even though there was a six-foot wall around the estate and the pool was hidden by trees. There was something wonderfully decadent about swimming nude at one in the morning. Aren't you coming in?"

He was already having trouble breathing, and he only shook his head. If he went in, he wouldn't do much swimming.

"And you said you weren't a pillar of the community." She laughed at him and trailed her fingers through the water. "All right, then, I guess I've got to get tough. It's for your own good." With a sigh, she lifted a hand out of the water. Like a child playing cowboy, she pointed it at him, finger out, thumb up. "Okay, Nathan, get up slow. Don't make any sudden moves."

"Give me a break, Jack."

"This is a hair trigger," she warned him. "Get up, and keep your hands where I can see them."

He couldn't have said why he did it. Maybe it was the full moon. He rose to a more interesting view.

"Okay, strip." She touched her tongue to her top lip. "Slow."

"You really are out of your mind."

"Don't beg, Nathan, it's pitiful." She cocked her thumb back over an invisible hammer. "Do you have any idea what a .38 slug can do to the human body? Take my word for it, it's not a pretty sight."

With a shrug, he pulled off his shirt. It wouldn't hurt to go in wearing his shorts. "You haven't got the guts to use that thing."

"Don't bet on it." But her lips twitched as she struggled with a grin. "Come a step closer with your pants on and I'll blow off a kneecap. Something like that gives a whole new meaning to the word *pain*."

She was crazy, he had no doubt about that. But apparently some of it had rubbed off. Nathan unsnapped his shorts and stepped out of them. She was going to get a surprise when he joined her in the water.

"That's good, very good." Deliberately she took her time evaluating him. "Now the rest."

With his eyes on hers, he stripped off his briefs. "You have no shame."

"Not a bit. Aren't you lucky?" Laughing, she gestured with her imaginary gun. "Into the pool, Nathan. Face the music."

He dived in, no more than an arm's length from her. When he surfaced, Jackie was treading water and smiling. "You dropped your gun."

She glanced down, as if surprised, at her open hand. "So I did."

"Let's see how tough you are unarmed."

He lunged for her, but she was quick. Anticipating him, Jackie dived deep, kicked out and glided under him. When she surfaced, she was six feet away with a smug smile. "Missed," she said lightly, and waited for his next move.

Slowly they circled, eyes locked. Jackie bit her lip, knowing that if she gave into the laughter she would be sunk in more ways than one. Nathan was as strong a swimmer as she, but she was counting on speed and agility to see her through. Until she was ready to lose.

He advanced, she evaded. He feinted, she adjusted. He maneuvered, she outmaneuvered. For the next few minutes there were only the sounds of insects and lapping water, giving them both a sense of solitude. Suddenly inspired, he brought a hand out of the water, cupping his fingers in his palm, pointing the index and cocking the thumb.

"Look what I found."

That was all it took to have her laughter breaking through. In two long strokes, he had her.

"Cheat. You cheated. Nathan, there's hope for you yet." Giggling, she reached to hug him. Then his hand was hard and fast around her hair. The roughness was so uncharacteristic that her eyes flew to his. What she saw had her breath catching. This time it was her mouth that went dry. "Nathan," she managed before her lips were imprisoned by his.

The need was fiercer, edgier, more frenzied than it had ever been before. He felt as though his body were full of springs that had all been wound too tightly. Against his own, her heart was beating desperately as he dived into her mouth, taking, tasting, devouring all. His teeth scraped her lips, his tongue invaded, tantalized by her breathless moan. Her body, at first taut as wire, went limp against him. They slipped beneath the surface without a thought for air.

The water enveloped them, making their movements slow and sluggish but no less urgent. The sensuous kiss of the cool, night-darkened water flowed around them, then ran off in torrents as they rose above it, still wrapped close.

Her first submission had passed. Now she was as desperate and anxious as he. She clung to him, head thrown back as he brought her up so that he could suckle her damp, water-cooled breasts. With each greedy pull, her stomach contracted and her pulse thudded out the new rhythm. The fingers on his shoulders dug in, leaving thin crescents. Then her mouth was on his again, thirsty.

She took her hands under, then over him, while her mind spun faster than her movements. Their bodies were captured in a slow-motion dreamworld, but their thoughts, their needs, raced.

Reaching down, he found her, cool and inviting. At his touch, his name burst from her. The sound of it across the quiet moonlight had his madness growing. She clung to him, her hands slipping over his slick body, then grasping for purchase. Her lips were wet and open when he took them again.

Jackie found her back braced against the side of the pool. Trembling with anticipation, she opened for him, then groaned when he filled her. Her hands fell lifelessly in the water, and he was there, holding her, moving in her.

The moonlight was on her face, making it both exotic and beautiful, but he could only press his own into her shoulder and ride the wave.

Chapter Eleven

Some people were born knowing how to entertain, and Jackie was one of them. The fact that she was using a party as a way of blocking out the knowledge that she had only a few more days until Nathan left didn't mean she was any less determined to make it a success.

She wrote for eight, sometimes ten, hours a day, losing herself in another romance, in another catastrophe. When she wasn't chained to her machine, she was shopping, planning menus, checking off lists and supplies.

She insisted on doing all the cooking herself but had decided to enlist Mrs. Grange to help serve and her son, the future teacher, to tend bar.

She was delighted when Nathan joined her in the kitchen the afternoon of the party, his sleeves rolled up and his mind set on helping her make hors d'oeuvres. Determined he was, and clumsy. Jackie found both traits endearing. Tactfully she buried his attempts on the bottom tray.

Jackie, optimistic about the weather, had planned to set up tables outside so that the guests could wander out among the colored lights she'd hung. Her faith was rewarded when the day remained clear and promised a star-filled, breezy night.

She rarely worried about the success or failure of a party, but this was different. She wanted it to be perfect, to prove to herself and to Nathan that she belonged in his world as much as she belonged in his arms.

She had only a matter of days left before he would fly thousands of miles away from her. It was difficult not to dwell on that, and on the fact that he had never told her what he wanted of her. What he wanted for them. She refused to believe that he still considered permanence impossible.

He'd never told her he loved her. That was a thought that hit her painfully at the oddest times. But he'd shown her in so many ways. Often he'd call her in the middle of the day just to hear her voice. He'd bring her flowers, from his garden or from a roadside stand, just when the ones she'd put in a vase had begun to fade. He'd draw her close, just to hold her after lovemaking, after passion had ebbed and contentment remained.

A woman didn't need words when she had everything else.

The hell she didn't.

Pushing back her gnawing doubts, Jackie told herself that for once she would have to be content with what she had instead of what she wanted.

An hour before the party she began to pamper herself. This was one of her mother's traditions that Jackie approved of. She was using her old room after telling Nathan he'd only be in her way. There was some truth in that, but more, Jackie had discovered she wanted to add a touch of mystery to the evening. She wanted him to see not the step-by-step preparation but the completed woman.

A long, leisurely bubble bath was first on her list. She soaked, the radio playing quietly while she looked out through the skylight over the tub. The only clouds in the sky were as harmless as white spun sugar.

She took time and care with her makeup, shooting for the exotic. When she studied her face from every angle in the mirror, she was satisfied with the results. She indulged in the feminine pleasure of slathering on perfumed cream before she took the dress she'd bought only the day before out of the closet.

Nathan was already downstairs when she started out. She could hear him talking to Mrs. Grange, and she could hear the woman's gruff replies. Always one to enjoy a bit of drama, Jackie put her hand on the rail and started slowly down.

She wasn't disappointed. Nathan glanced up, saw her and stopped in midsentence. Intent on him, she didn't notice the tall sandy-haired man beside Mrs. Grange. Nor did she see his mouth fall open.

Her eyes dominated her face, smudged on the lids with blending tones of bronze. Her hair, a combination of nature and womanly art, was windswept and cunningly tousled. Oversize silver stars glinted at her ears.

When Nathan could drag his gaze away from her face to take in the rest of her, it was another shock to the system.

The dress she'd chosen was stunning, eye-burning white that fell in a narrow column from her breasts to her ankles, leaving her shoulders bare and her arms unadorned but for the dozen silver bracelets that encircled her arm from her wrist almost to her elbow. Smiling, she reached the bottom, then turned in a circle, revealing the slit in the back of the dress that reached to midthigh.

"What do you think?"

"You're stunning."

Finishing the circle, she studied him in turn. No one wore a black suit with quite as much style as Nathan, Jackie thought. It must have been that broad-shouldered, muscled body that gave conservatism a dangerous look. She took a step closer to kiss him. Then, with her hand in his, she turned to Mrs. Grange.

"I really appreciate you helping us out tonight. And this is your son? You must be Charlie."

"Yes, ma'am." He swallowed audibly, then accepted the hand she offered. His palm was sweaty. His mother hadn't told him that Miss Jack was a goddess.

"It's nice to meet you, Charlie. Your mom's told us a lot about you. Shall I show you where we've set up the bar?"

Mrs. Grange gave him an elbow in the ribs. The boy looked as if he had rocks in his head when he stared that way. "I'll show him what he needs to know. Come on, Charlie, get the lead out."

Charlie went with his mother—because she had a death grip on his arm—but sent one last moonstruck look over his shoulder.

"The kid's eyes dropped on his shoes when he saw you."

With a laugh, Jackie tucked her arm through Nathan's. "That's kind of sweet."

"Mine hit the floor."

She looked at him, nearly level with him in her heeled sandals. "That's even sweeter."

"You always manage to surprise me, Jack."

"I hope so."

With his free hand he touched her shoulder, then ran his fingertips down her arm. "This is the first time I remember wishing a party was over before it began." It wasn't her usual scent tonight, but something stunningly sexy and taunting. "What did you do to yourself up there?"

"Tricks of the trade." She had to shift only slightly for her lips to meet his. "It's still me, Nathan."

"I know." His arm curled around her waist to keep her there. "That's why I wish the party was over."

"Tell you what." She slid her hands over his shoulders. "When it is, we'll have one all our own."

"I'm counting on it." He lowered his lips to hers as the doorbell rang.

"Round one," she said. Keeping his hand in hers, she went to answer the door.

Within an hour, the house was milling with people. Most of them were every bit as interested in finding out about the woman in Nathan's life as they were in an evening of socializing. She didn't mind. She was just as curious about them.

She discovered Nathan knew a wide variety of people, from the staunch and stuffy to the easygoing. It took only a smile and a greeting for her to click with Cody Johnson, an architect who had joined Nathan's firm two years before. He favored scuffed boots and faded jeans but had made a concession to formality by tossing on a suit jacket. Since her brother favored the same style and brand, Jackie recognized it as murderously expensive. He clamped a hand over hers, looked her up and down with eyes as brown as her own, then winked.

"I've been wanting to get a look at you."

"Check out the boss's outside interests?"

"Something like that." He still held her hand, but there was nothing flirtatious in the gesture. Jackie had the feeling that Cody got his impressions as much by touch as by sight. "One thing you can never fault Nathan for is his taste. I always figured whenever he looked more than twice at a woman she'd have to be special."

"That seemed like both a compliment and approval."

"You could say that." He didn't often give both so easily. "I'm glad, because Nathan's a good friend. The best. You planning on sticking around?"

Her brow lifted. Though she preferred direct questions, Jackie didn't feel obligated to respond with a direct answer. "You cut right through, don't you?"

"Hate to waste time."

Yes, she decided, she liked Cody Johnson just fine. With her hand still in his, she looked over and spotted Nathan. "I plan on sticking around."

His lips curved. He had one of those quick, arrogant grins that women found devastating. Because, Jackie thought, a woman could never be sure what he was thinking. "Then why don't I buy you a drink?"

Tucking her arm through his, she headed for the bar. "Have you met Justine Chesterfield?"

His laugh was full and rich. Jackie liked that as much as she did the sun-bronzed hair that fell over his forehead. "Anyone ever tell you you're clear as glass?"

"Hate to waste time."

"I appreciate that." He stopped at the bar and was amused by the way the college boy gaped at his hostess. "She's a nice lady, but a little rich for my blood."

"Is there anyone special?"

"Depends. You got a sister?"

With a laugh, Jackie turned and ordered champagne. Neither of them noticed Nathan watching them with a small, preoccupied frown.

He wasn't a jealous man. Nathan had always considered that one of the most foolish and unproductive emotions. Not only was jealousy the green-eyed monster, it invariably made the affected party look, and act, like an idiot.

He was neither an idiot nor jealous, but watching Jackie with Cody made him feel suspiciously like both. It was not, Nathan discovered, a sensation that could be enjoyed or ignored.

Cody was certainly more her type. Nathan managed to smile at the squeaky-voiced engineer who thought he had his attention. Cody could easily have passed for a gunfighter. Jackie's diamond-in-the-rough Jake Redman. That was Cody, with his loose limbed, rangy build and his sun-bleached hair that always looked as though it were one week past time for the barber. And there was the drawl. Nathan had always considered Cody's slight drawl soothing, but it began to occur to him that a woman might find it exciting. Some women.

Added to that was a deceptively laid-back attitude, a total lack of interest in convention and a restless, unerring eye for quality. Fast cars, late nights and bright lights. That was Cody.

When Nathan saw Jackie glance up and laugh into Cody's wide grin, he considered the potential satisfaction of strangling them both.

Ridiculous. Nathan sipped his drink, then reached for a cigarette. He wasn't fully aware that he rarely wanted—needed—a cigarette these days. Cody was a friend, probably the best friend Nathan had now, or had ever had. And Jackie... What was Jackie?

Lover, friend, companion. A delight and, oddly enough, a rock. It was strange to think of someone who looked and acted like a butterfly as something so solid and secure. She could be loyal when loyalty was deserved and strong when strength was needed. But rock or not, he'd given her no reason to pledge her fidelity. For her own good. He didn't want to cage her in or narrow her horizons.

The hell he didn't.

Cutting off the engineer in midsentence, Nathan made a vague excuse and moved toward Jackie.

She was laughing again, her face glowing with it, her eyes brilliant as they slanted upward over the rim of her champagne flute. "Nathan, you didn't tell me your associate was the kind of man mothers warn their daughters about." But as she spoke, her hand linked casually with Nathan's. It was the kind of ease that spoke of certain intimacy.

"I'm happy to take that as a compliment." Cody was drinking vodka straight up, and he toasted her with the squat glass. "Nice party, boss. I've already complimented you on your taste."

"Thanks. You know there are tables loaded with food outside. Knowing your appetite, I'm surprised you haven't found them."

"I'm on my way." He sent Jackie a final wink, then sauntered off.

"Well, that was certainly a subtle heave-ho," she commented.

"It seemed he was taking up a great deal of your time."

Her head swiveled around, her brows lifted, and then her face glowed again with a fresh smile. "That's nice. That's very, very nice." She brushed her lips lightly over his. "Some women don't care for possessive men. Myself, I like them a lot. To a point."

"I simply meant—"

"Don't spoil it." She kissed him again before she tucked her arm through his. "Well, shall we stroll around looking convivial, or shall we dive into that food before I starve to death?"

He raised her hand to his lips. The quick bout of jealousy, if that was what it was, hadn't caused him to look or act like an idiot. That was one more thing he'd have to rearrange his thinking about.

"We'll dive," he decided. "It's hard to be convivial on an empty stomach."

The evening was a complete success. Cards and calls came in over the next few days complimenting and commenting. Invitations were extended. It should have been a delightful time for Jackie. She had met Nathan's friends and associates and had won them over. But it wasn't Nathan's friends and associates who mattered. The bottom line was Nathan himself, and he was going to Denver.

It was no longer something she could think about later, not when his plane ticket was tucked in his briefcase. She'd been to Denver herself once, to sit on the fifty-yard line at Mile High Stadium and cheer. She'd enjoyed it well enough. Now she hated it, as a city and as a symbol.

He was leaving in a matter of hours, and they'd settled nothing. Once or twice he'd tried to talk to her, but she'd put him off. It was cowardly, but if he was going to brush her out of his life, she wanted every moment she could grab before it happened.

Now she was out of time, but she'd made herself a firm promise. He would at least tell her why. If he didn't want her any longer—wouldn't let himself want her—she would have the reasons.

She braced herself outside the bedroom door, squared her shoulders, then walked in. "I brought you some coffee."

Nathan glanced up from his packing. "Thanks." He'd thought he'd been miserable a few times before in his life. He'd been wrong.

"Need any help with this?" She lifted her own cup and sipped. Somehow it was easier to have serious, life-altering discussions when you were doing something as casual as drinking coffee.

"No. I'm almost finished."

Nodding, she sat on the edge of the bed. If she paced, as she wanted to, it would be easy to slam the cup against the wall and watch it shatter. As she wanted to. "You haven't said how long you'll be out of town."

"That's because I can't be sure." He'd never hated packing before. It had always been just one more small, slightly annoying chore. He hated it now. "It could be three weeks, more likely four, on this first trip. If we don't run into any major complications, I should be able to spot-check it as we go."

She sipped again, but the coffee was bitter. "Should I be here when you get back?"

It was like her to put it that way, not a demand or even a request, but a question. He wanted to say yes, please, yes, but "It's up to you" was what he told her.

"No, it's not. We both know how I feel, what I want. I haven't made a secret out of it." She paused a moment, wondering if she should feel a loss of pride. But none came. "Now it comes down to what you feel and what you want."

Her eyes were so solemn. There was no hint of a smile on her lips. He missed that, already missed that bright, vivid look she wore the way other women wore jewelry. "You mean a lot to me, Jackie." The word *love* was there, in his mind, in his heart, but he couldn't say it. "More than anyone else."

It amazed her that she was almost desperate enough, almost hungry enough, to accept those crumbs and be content. But she lifted a brow and continued watching him. "And?"

He packed another freshly laundered shirt. He wanted to choose the right words, say the right thing. Over and over during the last twenty-four hours he'd imagined what he would say to her, what he would do. In one wildly satisfying fantasy he'd dragged her to the airport with him and they'd flown away together. On a shell pelican.

But this was real. If he couldn't give her anything else, he could give her fairness.

"I can't ask you to stay, to wait, then live your life day by day. That's not what I want for you, Jack."

The hurting came from his honesty. He wouldn't lie or give her what she thought might be the comfort of pretense. "I'd like you to take a step back and tell me what you want for yourself. Is it what you had before, Nathan? Peace and quiet and no complications?"

Wasn't it? But somehow, when she said it, that life no longer sounded settled and comfortable, it sounded stagnant and boring. Yet it was the only one he was sure of. "I can't give you what you want," he said, struggling for calm. "I can't give you marriage and family and a lifetime commitment, because I don't believe in those things, Jack. I'd rather hurt you now than hurt you consistently over the rest of our lives."

She said nothing for a moment, afraid she would say too much. Her heart had gone out to him. There had been more misery in those last few words than she'd known he felt, or could feel. Though she hurt with him, she wasn't sorry she'd dredged it up.

"Was it that bad?" she said quietly. "Were you that unhappy growing up?"

He could have sworn at her for putting her slim, sensitive finger on the core of it. "That's not relevant."

"Oh, it is, and we both know it." She rose. She had to move, just a little, or the tension inside of her was going to explode and shatter her into a million pieces. "Nathan, I won't say you owe me an explanation. People are always saying 'he owes me,' or 'I owe him.' I've always felt that when you do something for someone, or give something away, that you should do it freely or not at all. So there's no debt." She sat again, calmer, then looked at him again. "But I have to say that I think it's right for you to tell me why."

He fished out a cigarette and lit it as he sat on the opposite end of the bed. "Yes, you're right. You're entitled to reasons." He was silent for a long time, trying to sort out the words, but it wasn't possible to plan them. So he simply began.

"My mother came from a wealthy and established family. She was expected to make a good marriage. A proper marriage. She'd been raised and educated with that in mind."

Jackie frowned a little, but tried to be fair. "That wasn't so unusual a generation ago."

"No, and it was the rule of thumb in her family. My father had more ambition than security, but had earned a reputation as an up-and-comer. He was, I've been told, dynamic and charismatic. When my mother fell in love with him, her family wasn't overjoyed, but they didn't object. Marriage to her gave my father exactly what he wanted. Family name, family backing, a well-bred wife who could entertain properly and give him an heir."

Jackie looked down at her empty cup. "I see," she murmured, and she was beginning to.

"He didn't love her. The marriage was a business decision."

He paused again, studying the column of smoke rising toward the ceiling. Was that the core of it? he wondered. Was that what had damaged his parents, and him, the most? Restless, he moved his shoulders. It was history, ancient history.

"I don't doubt that he had a certain amount of affection for her. He wasn't able, he'd never been able, to give too much of himself. His business took him away from home quite a bit. He was obsessed with making a fortune, with personal and professional success. When I was born, he gave my mother an emerald necklace as a reward for producing a son."

She started to speak, struck by the bitterness in his tone, then closed her mouth. Sometimes it was best only to listen.

"My mother adored him, was almost fanatic about it. As a child I had a nurse, a nanny and a bodyguard. She was terrified of what he might do if anything happened to me. It wasn't so much that she worried about me as a son, but as *his* son. His symbol."

"Oh, Nathan..." she began, but he shook his head.

"She told me in almost those words when I was five, six years old. She told me that and a great deal more once her feelings for him had changed. I rarely saw either of them when I was growing up. She was so determined to be the perfect society wife, and he was always flying off somewhere or another to close a deal. His idea of being a father consisted of periodic checks on my progress in school, lectures on responsibility and family honor. The trouble was, he had no honor himself."

With slow, deliberate motions he crushed out his cigarette. "There were other women. My mother knew and ignored it. He told me once there was nothing serious in those relationships. A man away from home so often required certain comforts."

"He told you?" Jackie demanded, stupidly shocked.

"When I was sixteen. I believe he considered it a heart-to-heart. My mother's feelings for him were dead by that time, and we were living like three polite strangers in the same house."

"Couldn't you have gone to your grandparents?"

"My grandmother was dead. She might have understood. I can't be sure. My grandfather considered the marriage a success. My mother certainly never complained, and my father had lived up to his potential. He would have been horrified if I'd arrived on his doorstep saying I couldn't live in the same house with my own parents. Besides, I had the place to myself a great deal of the time."

Privacy, she thought. She certainly understood his need for privacy. But what would it have done to a young boy to have his privacy in such an unhealthy place? "It must have been terrible for you."

She thought of her own family, wealthy, prestigious, respected. But their house had never been quiet, not the way she imagined Nathan's childhood home. It had never been cold. Hers had been filled with screams of laughter and accusations. With fists raised, the emotion in the threat heatedly real at the moment, then laughed about later.

"Nathan," she began slowly, "did you ever tell them how they made you feel?"

"Once. They were simply appalled with me for my lack of gratitude. And my lack of... graciousness in bringing up the subject. You learn not to beat your head against a wall that isn't going to move and find other ways."

"What other ways?"

"Study, personal ambitions. I can't say they ceased to exist for me as parents, but I shifted priorities. My father was away when I graduated from high school. I went to Europe that summer, so I didn't see him again until I was in college. He'd discovered I was studying architecture and came, he thought, to pull the rug out from under my feet.

"He wanted, as you put it once, for me to follow in his footsteps. He expected it. He demanded it. I'd lived under his thumb for eighteen years, totally cowed by my, and my mother's, perception of him. But something had happened. When I'd decided I wanted to build, the idea, the dream of that, became bigger than he."

"You'd grown up," she murmured.

"Enough, apparently, to stand up to him. He threatened to stop my tuition. I had a responsibility to him and the family business. That's all the family was, you see. A business. My mother was in full agree-ment. The fact was, once she'd stopped loving him, she couldn't have cared less. For her, I was my fa-ther's son."

"Surely that's too harsh, Nathan. Your mother—"

"Told me she hadn't wanted me." He reached for another cigarette, then broke it in half. "She said she believed if I hadn't been born her marriage could have been saved. Without the responsibility of a child she could have traveled with my father."

Her face had gone very white. She didn't want to believe him. She didn't want to think that anyone could be so cruel to her own child. "They didn't de-serve you." Swallowing a lump of tears, she rose to go to him.

"That's not the point." He put his hands out, knowing if she put her arms around him now he would fall apart. He had never spoken of this with anyone before, hadn't wanted to think it through stage by stage. "I made a decision that day I faced my father. I had no family, had never had one and didn't need one. My grandmother had left me enough to get me through college. So I used that, and took nothing from him. What I did from that point, I did on my own, for myself. That hasn't changed."

She let her arms rest at her sides. He wouldn't al-low her to comfort him, and as much as her heart ached to, her mind told her that perhaps it wasn't comfort he needed.

"You're still letting them run your life." Her voice wasn't soft now, but angry, angry with him, angry for him. "Their marriage was ugly, so marriage itself is ugly? That's stupid."

"Not marriage itself, marriage for me." Fury hit him suddenly. He'd opened up an old and tender wound for her, yet she still wanted more. "Do you think people only inherit brown eyes or a cleft chin from their parents? Don't you be stupid, Jack. They give us a great deal more than that. My father was a selfish man. I'm a selfish man, but at least I have the common sense to know I can't put myself, you or the children we'd have through that kind of misery."

"Common sense?" The MacNamara temper, famed for generations, leaped out. "You can stand there spouting off that kind of drivel and call it common sense? You haven't got enough sense to fill a tea-spoon. For God's sake, Nathan, if your father had been an ax murderer, does that mean you'd be lung-ing around looking for people to chop up? My father loves raw oysters, and I can't stand to look at them. Does that mean I'm adopted?"

"You're being absurd."

"I'm being absurd? *I'm* being absurd?" With a sound of disgust, she reached for the closest thing to hand—a nineteenth-century Venetian bowl—and smashed it to the floor. "You obviously wouldn't rec-ognize absurd if it shot you between the eyes. I'll tell you what's absurd. Absurd is loving someone and having them love you right back, then refusing to do anything solid about it because maybe, just maybe, it wouldn't work out perfectly."

"I'm not talking about perfect. Damn it, Jack, not that vase."

But it was already a pile of French porcelain shards on the floor. "Of course you're talking about per-fect. Perfect's your middle name. Nathan Perfect

Powell, projecting his life years into the future, making certain there aren't any loose ends or uneven edges."

"Fine." He swung her around before she could grab something else. "That should be enough right there to show you I'm right about this, about us. I like things done a certain way, I do plan ahead and insist on completing things as carefully as they're begun. You, by your own admission, never finish anything."

Her chin came up. Her eyes were dry. The tears would come later, she knew, torrents of them. "I wondered how long it would take you to throw that in my face. You're right about one thing, Nathan. The world's made up of two kinds of people, the careful and the careless. I'm a careless person and content to be so. But I don't think less of you for being a careful one."

He let out a quiet breath. He wasn't used to fighting, not unless it was over the quality of materials or working conditions for his men. "I didn't mean that as an insult."

"No? Well, maybe not, but the point's taken. We're not alike, and though I think we're both capable of a certain amount of growth and compromise, we'll never be alike. That doesn't change the fact that I love you and want to spend my life with you." This time she grabbed him, by the shirtfront. "You're not your father, Nathan, and I'm sure as hell not your mother. Don't let them do this to you, to us."

He covered her hands with his. "Maybe if you weren't so important it would be easier to risk it. I could say all right, we want each other, so let's take the chance. But I care for you too much to go into this with two strikes against me.''

"You care too much." The tears were going to come, and soon, so she backed away. "Damn you for that, Nathan. For not having the guts to say you love me, even now."

She whirled around and ran out. He heard the front door slam.

Chapter Twelve

The masons lost two days with the rain. I'm putting on double shifts.''

Nathan stood at the building site, squinting into the sun, which had finally made an appearance. It was cold in Denver. Spring hadn't floated in gently. The few hopeful wildflowers that had poked up had been carelessly trampled over. By next spring, the grounds would be green and trimmed. Looking at the scarred earth and the skeleton of the building, he already saw it.

''Considering the filthy weather you've been having, there's been a lot of progress in just under three weeks.'' Cody, a Stetson shading his eyes, his booted feet planted wide apart, looked at the beams and girders. Unlike Nathan, he didn't see the finished product. He preferred this stage, when there was still possibilities. "It looks good," he decided. "You, on the other hand, look like hell."

"It's always nice to have you around, Cody." Studying his clipboard, Nathan began a steady and detailed analysis of work completed and work projected. Schedules had to be adjusted, and deadlines met.

"You seem to have everything under control, as usual."

"Yeah." Nathan pulled out a cigarette, cupping his hands over his lighter.

As the flame leaped on, Cody noticed the shadows under Nathan's eyes, the lines of strain that had dug in around his mouth. To Cody's mind, there was only one thing that could make a strong man look battered. That was a woman.

Nathan dropped his lighter back in his pocket. "The building inspector should make his pass through today."

"Bless his heart." Cody helped himself to a cigarette from Nathan's pack. "I thought you were quitting these?"

"Eventually." One of the laborers had a portable radio turned up full. Nathan thought of Jackie blaring music through the kitchen speakers. "Any problems back home?"

"Businesswise? No. But I was about to ask you the same thing."

"I haven't been there, remember? Got an update on the Sydney project?"

"Ready to break ground in about six weeks." He took another drag, then broke the filter off the cigarette. Cody figured if you were going to kill yourself you might as well do it straight out. "You and Jack have a disagreement?"

"Why?"

"Because from the looks of you you haven't had a decent night's sleep since you got out here." He found a bent pack of matches in his pocket, remembered the club that was printed on the front with some fondness, then struck a match. "Want to talk about it?"

"There's nothing to talk about."

Cody merely lifted a brow and drew in more smoke. "Whatever you say, boss."

Nathan swore and pinched at the tension between his eyes. "Sorry."

"Okay." He stood quiet for a time, smoking and watching the men at work. "I could do with some coffee and a plateful of eggs." He pitched the stub of the cigarette into the construction rubble. "Since I'm on an expense account, I'll buy."

"You're a sport, Cody." But Nathan walked back to the pickup truck.

Within ten minutes they were sitting in a greasy little diner where the menu was written on a chalkboard and the waitresses wore holsters and short shocking-pink uniforms. There was a bald man dozing over his coffee at the counter and booths with ashtrays in the shape of saddles. The smell of onions hung stubbornly in the air.

"You always could pick a class joint," Nathan muttered as they slid into a booth, but all he could think of was how Jackie would have enjoyed it.

"It ain't the package, son." Cody settled back and grinned as one of the waitresses shrieked out an order to a stocky, grim-faced man at the grill.

A pot of coffee was plopped down without being asked for. Cody poured it himself and watched the steam rise. "You can keep your fancy French restaurants. Nobody makes coffee like a diner."

Jackie did, Nathan thought, and found he'd lost his taste for it.

Cody grinned up at the frowsy blonde who stopped, pad in hand, by their booth. "That blue plate special. I want two of them."

"Two blue plates," she muttered, writing.

"On one plate, darling," he added.

She looked over her pad and let her gaze roam over him. "I guess you do have a lot to fill up."

"That's the idea. Bring my friend the same."

She turned to study Nathan and decided it was her lucky day. Two hunks at her station, though the dark one looked as if he'd put in a rough night. Or a week of rough nights. She smiled at Nathan, showing crooked incisors. "How do you want your eggs, sweetie?"

"Over light," Cody told her, drawing her attention back to him. "And don't wring all the grease out of the home fries."

She chuckled and started off, her voice pitched high. "Double up on a couple of blue plates. Flip the eggs but make it easy."

For the first time in weeks, Nathan had the urge to smile. "What is the blue plate?"

"Two eggs, a rasher of bacon, home fries, biscuits and coffee by the barrel." As he took out one of his own cigarettes, Cody stretched his legs to rest his feet on the seat beside Nathan. "So, have you called her?"

It wasn't any use pretending he didn't want to talk about it. If that had been the case, he could have made some excuse and remained on the building site. He'd come because Cody could be counted on to be honest, whether the truth was pretty or not.

"No, I haven't called her."

"So you did have a fight?"

"I don't think you could call it a fight." Frowning, he remembered the china shattering on the floor. "No, you could call it that."

"People in love fight all the time."

Nathan smiled again. "That sounds like something she'd say."

"Sensible woman." He poured a second cup of coffee and noted that Nathan had left his untouched. "From the looks of you, I'd say whatever you two fought about, she won."

"No. Neither of us did."

Cody was silent for a moment, tapping his spoon on the table with the tinny country song playing on the jukebox. "My old man was big on sending flowers whenever he and my mother went at each other. Worked every time."

"This isn't as simple as that."

Cody waited until two heaping plates were set in front of them. He sent the waitress a cheeky wink, then dug in. "Nathan, I know you're the kind of man who likes to keep things to himself. I respect that. Working with you the last couple of years has been an education for me, in organization and control, in professionalism. But I figure by this time we're more than associates. A man has trouble with a woman, it usually helps if he dumps it out on another man. Not that another man understands women any better. They can just be confused about it together."

A semi pulled up in front of the diner's dusty window, gears groaning. "Jack wanted a commitment. I couldn't give her one."

"Couldn't?" Cody took his time pouring honey on a biscuit. "Isn't the word *wouldn't*?"

"Not in this case. For reasons I don't want to get into, I couldn't give her the marriage and family she wanted. Needed. Jack needed promises. I don't make promises."

"Well, that's for you to decide." Cody scooped up more eggs. "But it seems to me you're not too happy about it. If you don't love her—"

"I didn't say I didn't love her."

"Didn't you? Guess I misunderstood."

"Look, Cody, marriage is impossible enough when people think alike, when they have the same attitudes and habits. When they're as different as Jack and I, it's worse than impossible. She wants a home, kids and all the confusion that goes with it. I'm on the road for weeks at a time, and when I come home I want..." He let his words trail off because he no longer knew. He used to know.

"Yeah, that's a problem, all right," Cody continued as if Nathan weren't staring out of the window. "I guess dragging a woman along, having her to share those nameless hotel rooms and solitary meals, would be inconvenient. And having one who loved you waiting for you when you got home would be a pain."

Nathan turned back from the window and gave Cody a level look. "It would be unfair to her."

"Probably right. It's better to move on and be unhappy without her than risk being happy with her. Your eggs are getting cold, boss."

"Marriages break up as often as they work out."

"Yeah, the statistics are lousy. Makes you wonder why people keep jumping in."

"You haven't."

"Nope. Haven't found a woman mean enough." He grinned as he shoveled in the last of his eggs. "Maybe I'll look Jack up next week." The sudden deadly fury on Nathan's face had Cody stretching an arm over the back of the booth. "Figure this, Nathan, when a woman puts light into a man's life and he pulls the shade, he's asking for somebody else to enjoy it. Is that what you want?"

"Don't push it, Cody."

"No, I think you've already pushed yourself." He leaned forward again, his face quietly serious. "Let me tell you something, Nathan. You're a good man and a hell of an architect. You don't lie or look for the easy way. You fight for your men and for your principles, but you're not so hardheaded you won't compromise when it's time. You'll still be all of those things without her, but you could be a hell of a lot more with her. She did something for you."

"I know that." He shoved his all-but-untouched meal aside. "I'm worried about what I might do to her. If it were up to me..."

"If it were up to you, what?"

"It comes down to the fact that I'm not better off without her." That was a tough one to bring out in the open, to say plainly and live with. "But she may be better off without me."

"I guess she's the only one who can answer that." He drew out his wallet and riffled through bills. "I figure I know as much about this project here as you."

"What? Yes, so?"

"So I got an airline ticket in my room. Booked to leave day after tomorrow. I'll trade you for your hotel room."

Nathan started to make excuses, to give all the reasons why he was responsible for the project. Excuses, he realized, were all they would be. "Keep it," he said abruptly. "I'm leaving today."

"Smart move." Cody added a generous tip to the bill.

Nathan arrived home at 2:00 a.m. after a frenzied stop-and-go day of traveling. He'd had to route through St. Louis, bump into Chicago, then pace restlessly through O'Hare for two and a half hours waiting for his connection to Baltimore. From there he took his only option, a puddle jumper that touched down hourly.

He was sure she'd be there. He'd kept himself going with that alone. True, she hadn't answered when he'd called, but she could have been out shopping, in the pool, taking a walk. He didn't believe she'd left.

Somewhere in his heart he'd been sure all along that no matter what he'd said or how they'd left things she would be there when he returned. She was too stubborn and too self-confident to give up on him because he'd been an idiot.

She loved him, and when a woman like Jackie loved, she continued to love, for better or for worse.

He'd given her worse. Now, if she'd let him, he was going to try for better.

But she wasn't there. He knew it almost from the minute he opened his front door. The house had that same quiet, almost respectful feel it had had before she'd come into it. A lonely feel. Swearing, he took the steps two at a time, calling her.

The bed was empty, made up with Mrs. Grange's no-nonsense tucks. There were no colorful shirts or grubby shoes tossed anywhere. The room was neat as a pin. He detested it on sight. Still unable to accept it, he pulled open the closet. Only his own ordered clothes were there.

Furious with her, as well as himself, he strode into the guest room. And had to accept. She wasn't there, curled under tangled sheets. The clutter of books and papers was gone. So was her typewriter.

He stared for a long time, wondering how he could ever had thought it preferable to come home to order and peace. Tired, he sat on the edge of the bed. Her scent was still there, but it was fading. That was the worst of it, to have a trace of her without the rest.

He lay back on the bed, unwilling to sleep in the one he'd shared with her night after night. She wasn't going to get away with it, he thought, and instantly fell asleep.

"It's worse than pitiful for a grown man to cheat at Scrabble."

"I don't have to cheat." J.D. MacNamara narrowed his eyes and focused them on his daughter. "*Zuckly* is an adjective, meaning graceful. As in the ballerina executed a zuckly pirouette."

"That's a load of you-know-what," Jackie said, and scowled at him. "I let you get away with *quoho*, Daddy, but this is too much."

"Just because you're a writer now doesn't mean you know every word in the dictionary. Go ahead, look it up, but you lose fifty points if you find it."

Jackie's fingers hovered over the dictionary. She knew her father could lie beautifully, but she also knew he had an uncanny way of coming out on top. With a sigh of disgust, she dropped her hand. "I'll concede. I know how to be a zuckly player."

"That's my girl." Pleased with himself, he began to add points to his score. Jackie lifted her glass of wine and considered him.

J.D. MacNamara was quite a man. But then, she'd always known that. She supposed it was Nathan's description of his own father, his family life, that had made her stand back and appreciate fully what she'd been given. She knew her father had a tough-as-nails reputation in the business world. He derived great pleasure from wheeling and dealing and outwitting competitors. Yet she'd seen the same self-satisfied look on his face after pulling off a multimillion-dollar business coup as she saw on it now as he outscored his daughter in a game of Scrabble.

He just loved life, with all its twists and turns. Perhaps Nathan was right about children inheriting more than eye color, and if she'd inherited that joie de vivre from her father, she was grateful.

"I love you, Daddy, even if you are a rotten cheat."

"I love you, too, Jackie." He beamed at the totals. "But I'm not going to let that interfere with destroying you. Your turn, you know."

Folding up her legs, she propped her elbows and stared owlishly at her letters. The room was gracefully lit, the drapes yet to be drawn as sunset exploded in the eastern sky. The second parlor, as her mother insisted on calling it, was for family or informal gatherings, but it was a study in elegance and taste.

The rose-and-gray pattern of the Aubusson was picked up prettily in soft floor-length drapes and the upholstery of a curvy sofa. Her mother's prize collection of crystal had been moved out some years before when Jackie and Brandon had broken a candy dish while wrestling over some forgotten disagreement. Patricia had stubbornly left a few dainty pieces of porcelain.

There was a wide window seat in the east wall, where Jackie had hidden playing hide-and-seek as a child and dreamed of her latest crush as a teenager. She'd spent thousands of hours in that room, happy ones, furious ones, tearful ones. It was home. She hadn't fully understood or appreciated that until now.

"What's the matter with you, girl? Writers are supposed to have a way with words."

Her lips twitched a bit. J.D. had already fallen into the habit of calling her a writer several times a day. "Off my case, J.D."

"Hell of a way to talk to your father. Why, I ought to take a strap to you."

She grinned. "You and who else?"

He grinned back. He had a full, generous face with that oh-so-Irish ruddy skin. His eyes were a bright blue even through the glasses he had perched on his nose. He wore a suit because dressing for dinner was expected, but the vest was unbuttoned and the tie pulled crooked. A cigar was clamped between his big teeth, a cigar that Patricia tolerated in dignified silence.

Jackie pushed her letters around. "You know, Daddy, I've just began to think about it, but you and Mother, you're so different."

"Hmmm?" He glanced up, distracted from the creative demands of inventing a new word.

"I mean, Mother is so elegant, so well groomed."

"What am I, a slob?"

"Not exactly." When he frowned, she spread out her letters on the board. "There, *hyfoxal*."

"What the hell is this?" J.D. waved a blunt finger at the word. "No such thing."

"It's from the Latin for sly or cleverly adept. As in 'My father is well-known for his hyfoxal business dealings."

In answer, J.D. used a brief four-letter word that would have had his wife clucking her tongue. "Look it up," Jackie invited. "If you want to lose fifty points. Daddy," she said to distract him again, "how do you and Mother stay so happy?"

"I let her do what she does best, she lets me do what I do best. Besides, I'm crazy about the old prude."

"I know." Jackie felt her eyes fill with the tears that never seemed far away these days. "I've been thinking a lot lately about what you've both done for me and the boys. And loving each other might be the most important part of all."

"Jack, why don't you tell me what's on your mind?"

She shook her head but leaned over to stroke his cheek. "I just grew up this spring. Thought you'd like to know."

"And does growing up have anything to do with the man you're in love with?"

"Just about everything. Oh, you'd like him, Daddy. He's strong, sometimes too strong. He's kind and funny in the oddest sorts of ways. He likes me the way I am." The tears threatened again, and she put a hand to her eyes, pressing hard for a moment. "He makes lists for everything and always makes sure that *B* follows *A*. He, uh..." Letting out a long breath, she dropped her hands. "He's the kind of man who opens the door for you, not because he thinks it's the gentlemanly or proper thing to do, but because he is a gentleman. A very gentle man." She smiled again, her tears under control. "Mother would like him, too."

"Then what's the problem, Jackie?"

"He's just not ready for me or for the way we feel about each other. And I'm not sure how long I can wait for him to get ready."

J.D. frowned a moment. "Want me to give him a kick in the pants?"

That made her laugh. She was up and in his lap, her arms tight around him. "I'll let you know."

Patricia glided into the room, slim and pretty in a silk sheath the same pale blue as her eyes. "John, if the chef continues to throw these disgraceful temper tantrums, you're going to have to speak to him yourself. I'm at my wit's end." She went to the bar, poured a small glass of dry sherry, then settled in a chair. She crossed her legs, which her husband still considered the best on the East Coast, and sipped. "Jackie, I came across a new hairdresser last week. I'm convinced he could do wonders for you.''

Jackie grinned and blew her hair out of her eyes. "I love you, Mother."

Instantly, and in the way Jackie had always adored, Patricia's eyes softened. "I love you too, darling. I meant to tell you that your tan is wonderfully flattering, particularly with your coloring, but after all I've been reading lately I'm worried about the long-term effects." Then she smiled in a way that made her look remarkably like her daughter. "It's good to have you home for a little while. The house is always too quiet without you and the boys."

"Won't be seeing too much of her now." J.D. gave her a fatherly pinch on the rump. "Now that she's a big-time author."

"It's only one book," she reminded him, then grinned. "So far."

"It did give me a great deal of satisfaction to mention, very casually, of course, to Honoria that you'd sold your manuscript to Harlequin Historicals." Patricia took a delicate sip as she settled back on the cushions.

"Casual?" J.D. gave a shout of laughter. "She couldn't wait to pick up the phone and brag. Hey, there, what do you think you're doing?"

Jackie turned back from her study of his letters. "Nothing." She gave him a loud kiss on the cheek. "You're doomed, you know. You're never going to be able to use that ridiculous collection."

"We'll see about that." J.D. dumped her off of his lap, then rubbed his palms together. "Sit down and shut up."

"John, really," Patricia said, in a tone that had Jackie running over to hug her. When the doorbell rang, Jackie straightened, but her mother waved her back. "Philip will get the door, Jacqueline. Do fix your hair."

Dutifully Jackie dragged her fingers through it as their graying butler came to the parlor entrance. "I beg your pardon, Mrs. MacNamara, but there's a Nathan Powell here to see Miss Jacqueline."

With a quick squeal, Jackie leaped forward. Her mother's firm command stopped her. "Jacqueline, sit down and pretend you're a lady. Philip will show the man in."

"But—"

"Sit down," J.D. told her. "And shut up."

"Quite," Patricia murmured, then nodded to Philip.

She sat with a thud.

"And I'd take that sulky look off your pointy face," her father suggested. "Unless you want him to turn right around and leave again."

Jackie gritted her teeth, glared arrows at him, then settled down. Maybe they were right, she thought. Just this once, she'd look before she leaped. But when she saw him she would have been out of her chair in an instant if her father's foot hadn't stamped down on hers.

"Jack." There was something strained and husky about his voice, as though he hadn't spoken for days.

"Hello, Nathan." Pulling herself in, she rose easily and offered a hand. "I didn't expect you."

"No, I . . ." He felt suddenly and completely foolish standing there in a travel-stained suit with a brightly ribboned box under his arm. "I should have called."

"Of course not." As if there had never been any strain between them, or any passion, she tucked her arm through his. "I'd like you to meet my parents. J.D. and Patricia MacNamara, Nathan Powell."

J.D. shoved himself to his feet. He'd already made his assessment, and if he'd ever seen a more lovesick, frustrated man before, he couldn't bring it to mind. It was with both sympathy and interest that he offered a hand.

"Pleased to meet you. Admire your work." He shook his hand with a hefty pumping stroke. "Jack's told us all about you. I'll get you a drink."

Nathan managed to nod through these rapid-fire statements before turning to greet Jackie's mother. This was what she would look like in twenty or twenty-five years, Nathan realized with a jolt. Still lovely, with her skin clear as a bell and the grace that only years could add.

"Mrs. MacNamara, I apologize for dropping in on you like this."

"No need for that." But it pleased her that he had the manners to do so. She took stock in much the same way her husband had and saw a breeding and a kindness that she approved of. "Won't you sit down, Mr. Powell?"

"Well, I—"

"Here you are, nothing like a nice shot of whiskey to put hair on your chest." J.D. slapped him on the back as he offered the glass. "So you design buildings? Do any remodeling?"

"Yes, when there's—"

"Good, good. I'd like to talk to you about this building I'd had my eye on. Place is a mess, but it has potential. Now if I—"

"Excuse me." Forgetting his manners, Nathan shoved the glass back in J.D.'s hand and grabbed Jackie's arm. Without another word, he dragged her through the terrace doors he'd spotted.

"Well." Patricia raised both brows as if scandalized and hid her smile in her drink. J.D. merely hooted and downed the whiskey himself.

"Up to planning a wedding, Patty, old girl?"

The air was balmy and full of flowers. The stars were close enough to touch, vying with the moon for brilliance. Nathan noticed none of it as he stopped, dropped his package on a gleaming white table and hauled Jackie into his arms.

She fit perfectly.

"I'm sorry," he managed after a moment. "I was rude to your parents."

"That's all right. We often are." She lifted both hands to his face and studied him. "You look tired."

"No, I'm fine." He was anything but. Searching for lost control, he stepped back. "I wasn't sure you'd be here, either."

"Either?"

"You were gone when I got home, and then I tracked down your apartment, but you weren't there, either, so I came looking here."

Hoping she could take it slowly, she leaned back against the table. "You've been looking for me?"

"For a couple of days."

"I'm sorry. I didn't expect you back from Denver until next week. Your office certainly didn't."

"I came back sooner than— You called my office?"

"Yes. You came back sooner than what, Nathan?"

"Sooner than expected," he said with a snap. "I left Cody in charge, dumped the project in his lap and flew home. You'd gone. You'd left me."

She nearly flew at him, laughing, but decided to play it out. "Did you expect me to stay on?"

"Yes. No. Yes, damn it." He dragged both hands through his hair. "I know I hadn't any right to expect it, but I did. Then, when I got home, the house was empty. I hated it there without you. I can't think without you. That's your fault. You've done something to my brain." He'd begun to pace, which made her lift a brow. The Nathan she'd come to know rarely made unnecessary moves. "Every time I see something I wonder what you'd think about it, what you'd say. I couldn't even eat a blue plate special without thinking about you."

"That's really dreadful." She drew a breath. It needed to be asked. "Do you want me back, Nathan?"

There was fury in his eyes when he turned, a kind of vivid, blazing fury that made her want to launch herself into his arms again. "Do you want me to crawl?"

"Let me think about it." She touched the bow on the package, wondering what was inside. Wondering was almost as good as knowing. "You deserve to crawl a bit, but I don't have the heart for it." She smiled at him, her hands folded neatly. "I hadn't gone anywhere, Nathan."

"You'd cleared out. The place was tidy as a tomb."

"Didn't you look in the closet?"

Impatience shimmered, then stilled. "What do you mean?"

"I mean, I hadn't left. My clothes are still in the guest room. I couldn't sleep in your bed without you, so I moved, but I didn't leave." She touched his face again, gently. "I had no intention of letting you ruin your life."

He grabbed her hand as if it were a lifeline. "Then why are you here and not there?"

"I wanted to see my parents. Partly because of the things you'd told me. It made me realize I needed to see them, to thank them somehow for being as wonderful as they are. And partly because I wanted to tell them I'd finally done something from beginning to end." Her fingers curved nervously over his. "I sold my book."

"Sold it? I didn't know you'd sent it in."

"I didn't want to tell you. I didn't want you to be disappointed in me if it didn't work."

"I wouldn't have been." He drew her close. Her scent, so needed, was all around him. It was only then that he understood that you could come home even without the familiar walls. "I'm happy for you. I'm proud of you. I wish . . . I wish I'd been here."

"This is something I had to do, this first time, by myself." She shifted back, not out of his arms, but circled by them. "I'd like you to be around the next time."

His fingers tensed on the back of her waist, and his eyes went dark. Jake's look, she thought yet again, giddy with love for him. "It's that easy? All I had to do was walk in and ask?"

"That's all you've ever had to do."

"I don't deserve you."

She smiled. "I know."

With a laugh, he swung her in a circle, then brought her down to crush his lips to hers in a long, breathless kiss. "I came prepared to make all kinds of offers and promises. You aren't going to ask for any."

"That's not to say I wouldn't like to hear them." She laid her head on his shoulder. "Why don't you tell me what you've got in mind?"

"I want you, but I want it to be right. No long separations, no broken promises. I'm doing something I should have done a year ago and making Cody a partner."

When she drew her head back, he noticed that her eyes could be as shrewd as her father's. "That's an excellent decision."

"A personal one, as well as a business one. I'm learning, Jack."

"I can see that."

"Between the two of us, the pressure will lighten enough to make it possible to start a family, a real family. I don't know what kind of husband I'll make, or father, but—"

She touched her fingers to his lips. "We'll find out together."

"Yes." Reaching up, he took her hands again. "I'll still have to travel some, but I hope you'll agree to come with me whenever you can."

"Just try to stop me."

"And you'll be there to make certain I don't forget that marriage and family come first."

She turned her face into his throat. "You can count on it."

"I'm doing this backward. I do that a lot since I met you." He ran his hands down her arms, then drew her away. "I wanted to tell you that since I found you everything changed for me. Losing you would be worse than losing my eyes or my arms, because without you I can't see or touch anything. I need you in my life, I want you to share it all with me. We can learn from each other, make mistakes together, and I love you more than I know how to say."

"I think you said it very nicely." She sniffled, then shook her head. "I don't want to cry. I look really awful when I cry, and I want to be beautiful tonight. Let me have my present, will you, before I start babbling?"

"I like it when you babble." He pressed a kiss to her brow, to her temple, to the dimple at the corner of her mouth. "Oh, God, I do owe cousin Fred."

Jackie gave a watery laugh. "He's trying to find a buyer for twenty-five acres of swampland."

"Sold." He caught her face in his hands again, just to look, just to touch what was more real to him than his own heart. "I do love you, Jack."

"I know, but you can repeat yourself all you want."

"I intend to, but first I think you should have this." He picked up the package and offered it to her. "I wanted you to have something that would show you, if I couldn't make myself clear, how I felt about you. How you'd given me hope for a future I never believed in."

She dragged the heels of her hands under her eyes. "Well, let's see. Diamonds are forever, but I've always had a fondness for colored stones.'' She ripped at the paper ruthlessly, then pulled out her gift.

For a moment she was speechless, standing in the moonlight, her cheeks still gleaming with tears. In her hands was a shell-covered pelican. When she looked at him again, her eyes were drenched. ''Nobody understands me the way you do.''

''Don't change,'' he murmured, holding her close again with the tacky bird between them. ''Let's go home, Jack.''

* * * * *

Keepsake

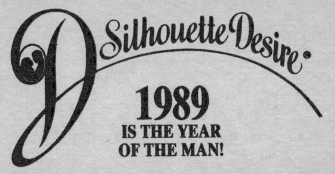

Silhouette Desire ®

1989
IS THE YEAR
OF THE MAN!

What makes a romance? A special man, of course, and Silhouette Desire celebrates that fact with *twelve* of them! From Mr. January to Mr. December, every month spotlights the Silhouette Desire hero—our **MAN OF THE MONTH.**

Sexy, macho, charming, irritating…irresistible! Nothing can stop these men from sweeping you away. Created by some of your favorite authors, each man is custom-made for pleasure—*reading* pleasure—so don't miss a single one.

Diana Palmer kicks off the new year, and you can look forward to magnificent men from **Joan Hohl**, **Jennifer Greene** and many, many more. So get out there and find your man!

Silhouette Desire's

MAN OF THE MONTH...

MAND-1

ATTRACTIVE, SPACE SAVING BOOK RACK

Display your most prized novels on this handsome and sturdy book rack. The hand-rubbed walnut finish will blend into your library decor with quiet elegance, providing a practical organizer for your favorite hard-or soft-covered books.

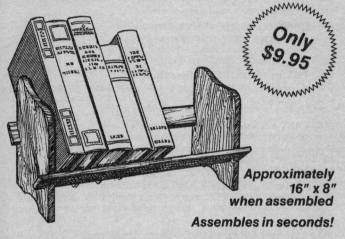

Only $9.95

Approximately 16" x 8" when assembled

Assembles in seconds!

To order, rush your name, address and zip code, along with a check or money order for $10.70* ($9.95 plus 75¢ postage and handling) payable to *Silhouette Books*.

Silhouette Books
Book Rack Offer
901 Fuhrmann Blvd.
P.O. Box 1396
Buffalo, NY 14269-1396

Offer not available in Canada.

BKR-2A

*New York and Iowa residents add appropriate sales tax.

Silhouette Special Edition

COMING NEXT MONTH

#505 SUMMER'S PROMISE—Bay Matthews
Burdened with grief, Joanna felt empty, old, weary of living. But when her estranged husband, Chase, appeared on her doorstep, need and desire took hold...and a new life began.

#506 GRADY'S LADY—Bevlyn Marshall
Ladies' man Ryan Grady had tangled with Blythe Peyton's type before—blond, beautiful, deadly. He had to protect his brother from her poison, no matter how sweet it tasted....

#507 THE RECKONING—Joleen Daniels
Once, Cal Sinclair had offered her an ultimatum. Laura Wright had chosen college over marriage...and Cal had chosen Laura's sister. Could heated passion ever sear away burning regrets?

#508 CAST A TALL SHADOW—Diana Whitney
Juvenile investigator Kristin Price was gutsy, but a harrowing stint on Nathan Brodie's ranch for delinquents truly tested her courage. Even for love's sake, could she confront her most intimate terrors?

#509 NO RIGHT OR WRONG—Katherine Granger
Single mother Anne Emerson didn't need another man—or another scandal—messing up her life, and her best friend's ex-husband was a candidate for both. Somehow, though, being wrong had never felt so right.

#510 ASK NOT OF ME, LOVE—Phyllis Halldorson
Was Caleb's past too dangerous to speak of—even to his love? What terrible secret had made him dodge Nancy's questions and desert her in a time of need?

AVAILABLE THIS MONTH:

#499 LOVING JACK
Nora Roberts

#500 COMPROMISING POSITIONS
Carole Halston

#501 LABOR OF LOVE
Madelyn Dohrn

#502 SHADES AND SHADOWS
Victoria Pade

#503 A FINE SPRING RAIN
Celeste Hamilton

#504 LIKE STRANGERS
Lynda Trent